MW00512576

BOOKF
Turner, Lynn M.
Adieu, my love /

SEP 2 3 2009			

MASONVILLE
BRANCH LIBRARY

ADIEU, MY LOVE

Other books by Lynn M. Turner:

Cutter's Wake
Growing Attraction

ADIEU, MY LOVE

•

Lynn M. Turner

AVALON BOOKS
NEW YORK

© Copyright 2007 by Lynn M. Turner
All rights reserved.
All the characters in this book are fictitious,
and any resemblance to actual persons,
living or dead, is purely coincidental.

Published by Thomas Bouregy & Co., Inc.
160 Madison Avenue, New York, NY 10016

Library of Congress Cataloging-in-Publication Data

Turner, Lynn M.
   Adieu, my love / Lynn M. Turner.
         p.   cm.
   ISBN 978-0-8034-9836-5 (hardcover : acid-free paper)
1. Nova Scotia—History—1713–1763—Fiction.   2.
Louisbourg (N.S.)—Fiction.   I. Title.

    PR9199.3.T837A35 2007
    813'.6—dc22

                                        2007003749

PRINTED IN THE UNITED STATES OF AMERICA
ON ACID-FREE PAPER
BY HADDON CRAFTSMEN, BLOOMSBURG, PENNSYLVANIA

To my good friend, Cindy T. Moss.
All these years later . . .

Lynn M. Turner wishes to acknowledge that the Province of Nova Scotia, through the Department of Tourism, Culture and Heritage, provided support during the creation of this novel.

Tourism, Culture and Heritage

Chapter One

On a gleaming spring day in 1751, Matthew Carter squinted across the water toward sharp spires rising above a grassy mound, silhouetted against the wash of blue sky: Louisbourg, the French stronghold of coastal North America, a rope in the tug-of-war between France and England since 1713. His shoulders hunched and the hairs on his forearms bristled, whether from the damp cold or a deep fear he didn't know. It made no difference. He would be marooned here on this rocky outcrop, teetering on the edge of the icy North Atlantic, trapped by a thoughtless whim, an impulsive statement made many months ago.

Behind him the crew of the *Conquerant* scurried over the rigging, responding to the gruff hollers from the deck, fighting to bring the frigate through the narrow channel of Louisbourg Harbor. Matthew braced his feet as the ship leaned against the wind and came around. His thigh muscles, hardened by the months at sea, took his weight first on one leg then the other.

Throughout the morning he'd caught whiffs of a pungent smell, like a pickle barrel mixed with cooking cabbage. Now he understood why. Miles of fish lay drying in jagged rows around the shoreline, some on tables, others on the bare smooth rock. Cod. That's why they were all here, the soldiers, the fishermen, the merchants, even Matthew himself. The town clung to this rocky wilderness because of the cod stocks. Wars and death and the possibility of incredible wealth, all for a stinking fish.

The ship glided past a grassy island then slid between a headland on the right, dominated by a tall white lighthouse, and a low battery island on the left. Matthew strained to commit everything he saw to memory—where the guns were placed, how high the cliffs rose, and where they were scalable. More than a hundred vessels were moored in the large harbor: warships, schooners, and shallops—a field of slender masts poking up like knitting needles. Beyond them towered the massive walls and battlements of the fortress.

There it lay. Louisbourg. It commanded a peninsula cupping the harbor, rising on a gentle slope. Although modest compared to the fortifications Matthew had studied in Europe, it felt impressive here on the edge of this sparsely populated continent. The town behind the walls looked tidy, with a mix of wooden and stone houses and warehouses all on a grid of streets. Long buildings dominated the eastern end, near a substantial land gate. Here and there openings toothed into the chest-high sea wall, where tenders offloaded barrels, chests, and canvas blocks onto ramps slanting up from the water.

One of Matthew's fellow captives poked a sharp elbow into his side. Tom Smith was a short, skinny man past his youth but still wiry, with bushy blond eyebrows and deep lines on his tanned face. His gold earring sparkled in the sun. He spoke with the twang of his New England heritage. "You ain't never been here before, huh?"

"Never."

"See them two pointy things," Tom said, motioning toward the town. "That one over yonder is the hospital, and that one at the top of the hill is the King's Bastion."

Outside the fortress walls an unending string of ragged structures crowded the shoreline: wooden houses with grass roofs, fish shingles sagging under the weight of drying cod, and short docks cobbled from uneven logs. Only a smattering of buildings dotted the treeless hills to the north on the landward side of the harbor.

"It's a big town," Matthew said.

"Aye, it is that. Plenty of grog shops, and I've been in them all." He cocked his head and spat into the water. "I never been here as a prisoner before. Don't like it none, neither."

"Were you here for the siege?" Matthew tensed, waiting for the answer.

"Naw. My nephew was though. He was some mad when they gave this place back to France."

"I understand the New Englanders ransacked the town after the surrender."

"Not so much. Fact is, they fixed up a lot of the buildings during the occupation. Had it all spiffy for when the French came strolling back in. Went a long way to getting rid of the bad feelings." Tom shook his head, then added, "Can't for the life of me figure why they arrested us this time."

"We *were* smuggling," Matthew snapped.

Tom shrugged. "So? Everybody does it. Ain't never caused a ruckus before now."

"We are enemies, the French and the English."

"Funny hearing that coming from you, what with that Frenchie way you talk." He held up a callused hand to stop Matthew from explaining how he came to be a Frenchman living in New England. "I know, I know," Tom said. "You ain't no Catholic."

At that thought, Tom jabbed a finger toward the town again. "Wait till ya sees the church they got here. Whew, all painted up with gold and the like. Come to think of it, we'll see it all right." He gave a phlegm-filled chuckle. "They got the prison right across the hall."

Matthew squeezed his eyes shut. *Prison.* What had he gotten himself into?

Marie-Charlotte Jubert forced herself to move more sedately than her usual brisk stride as she worked her way around the crowd and down the packed earth of the quay toward the bakery. She carried a tray heavy with loaves of bread and didn't want to jostle the dough. She'd kneaded them the night before, formed the loaves, and carved the tops with her own symbol, a double loop like a ribbon's bow. After a night rising next to the banked fire, the mounds swelled to tender heights and smelled of pungent yeast. Like many of her neighbors, Marie brought her loaves to the bakery to be fired in its massive ovens.

"Good morning, Madame Jubert."

"Good morning, Monsieur." Marie, recognizing the man by his Basque accent, responded without looking around. It didn't surprise her to find Jean Riverin in town this early; he was the master of one of her shore crews and didn't get busy until the fishermen returned with the day's catch. He had rosy cheeks under a dark tan, a long nose, and black hair curling from under his toque. Many of the young girls in town thought him swarthy and handsome despite the fact that he smelled of brine. Marie could see the attraction—she wasn't blind, just uninterested.

Further along the quay Paulette Maigny sat on a narrow bench in a spot of sunlight, picking in a bored way at the white ribbon hanging from her cap. In her feminine yellow dress, she looked like a bright flower against the granite of the wall behind her and the packed earth under her feet. Marie thought Paulette's clothing too impractical and frivolous, with wasteful yards of too-fine fabric. Paulette continually nagged Marie to wear more flattering attire, something other than bleached aprons and dull linen.

"Good day, Paulette."

"Oh, Marie," Paulette chirped. "You've heard, then?"

"Heard what?" Marie's arms ached from the weight of the loaves.

Paulette waved a hand toward the harbor. "The *Conquerant*, she's back."

"And why would I care?" Marie asked, more out of habit than indifference.

"You're not curious about why he left in such a hurry?" Paulette lifted her billowing skirts and started across the quay and up the packed earth bank toward the sea wall.

"I'm sure we'll find out soon enough. I have to get—"

"Come on!"

Marie made a dismissive sound in her throat. The girl had no responsibilities and no concept of what it took to keep a business on schedule day after day. It wasn't her fault, of course. Her wealthy and indulgent parents, saving her for a good match, kept the nineteen-year-old firmly in hand.

"But isn't that . . . ?" Paulette called over her shoulder and pointed toward the harbor. "Isn't that the *Donna Rae*?"

That stopped Marie. The *Donna Rae* should have been halfway to Halifax by now.

"Come and look."

Marie shifted the tray in her arms. "It can't be."

"It is the *Donna Rae*, I tell you."

"What a waste of time," she snapped, even though her shoulders tightened. She clambered up the bank and carefully balanced the tray on the moss-covered planks over the sea wall. The white coverlet fluttered in the cool breeze, so she tucked it close to the bread while peering past the nearer vessels to the east. When her gaze landed on the schooner, her breath caught in her throat. The *Donna Rae*, her beautiful schooner.

Marie didn't own the vessel outright—she had secret partners in New England—but she loved it as if it were her own. How could she not? The *Donna Rae* sang across the water like a lilting melody, her pretty lines complementing every cloud, every ocean swell, every curve of the land. The schooner worked hard too, lugging cargo up and down the coastline virtually twelve months of the year.

"She's riding deep," Marie mumbled, watching it tack closer to shore. That meant that the *Donna Rae* had already visited Canso and picked up her cargo—smuggled cargo. The schooner was to have met a larger ship coming from Europe and offload her sailcloth and wines, which she would then carry down the coast to Marie's secret English partners.

It was illegal for a merchant to carry on unsupervised trade with the English. On the other hand, not yet self-sufficient, Louisbourg needed things like bricks and tools from New England, so the government allowed a smidgen of strictly regulated commerce, all of it snarled in tortuous red tape, expensive permits, and licenses. They sucked the profit away. And that wasn't the worst. Every time a vessel entered or left the harbor, officials boarded her to compose lengthy reports on the cargo and every person on board. If it was a foreign cargo or ship, they posted a guard. The cost for all this landed on the merchant's desk, of course.

Marie-Charlotte Jubert was no fool. She exchanged cargoes in a harbor south of Canso and sailed around the red tape, as did a dozen other Louisbourg merchants. The officials usually turned a blind eye because many of them either had a hand in the smuggling or were leery of antagonizing powerful merchants who had influence back in France. Even so, no one dared to conduct the smuggling right here in Louisbourg; that asked for trouble. Although some of her friends and associates suspected that Marie had a hand in the business, only one other person in the town knew for sure: Quentin Bauldry, her foreman.

Why was her schooner here? Marie clenched her fists. She couldn't lose the *Donna Rae*. It would be a disaster. She felt like commandeering the nearest tender and rowing out to find out what had gone wrong. But she had to keep calm, to act as if she didn't care at all about the vessel.

"You say the *Conquerant* is here as well?" she asked through the tightness in her throat. Was it a coincidence the two vessels arrived at the same time?

"There."

The frigate moored in a choice place, just off the Frederic Gate. A crew of men scampered up and down the four masts and rigging, hauling up the square sails. Meanwhile, down at the water a tender pushed off the hull. It was easy to pick out Capitaine Jerome de Monluc in his officer's uniform. He sat in the prow, straight-backed, tricorne hat secured under his elbow, looking supremely self-satisfied. Marie turned back toward the *Donna Rae* and prayed there was no connection.

Was the schooner damaged? Perhaps that was why she put into port. She seemed to maneuver well enough. Or a medical emergency with one of her crew? Or with someone in Canso? Even if that were the case, Captain Martin wouldn't risk coming right into harbor; he'd hire a fishing boat to carry the man in.

Marie grabbed her tray and hurried across to the tall masonry house, up the four steps, and into the front room. She had to get rid of this bread. Inside the air smelled delicious with baking sweets and yeast, but the heat quickly brought dampness to her forehead.

"Good day, Madame Jubert." Madame Brunet, the proprietor, ran her hands down her striped apron. She was a short, chubby woman who always seemed to be moving. "I hear the *Conquerant* is back."

"Why would I be interested?" Marie snapped. She slid the tray along a rack.

"One would think . . ." Madame Brunet finished with an expressive shrug, not the least flustered by Marie's tone.

Marie knew what people thought, but she had no intention of becoming the wife of Capitaine Jerome de Monluc, the old prig. She was about to announce that to Madame Brunet, but instead she let out an exasperated, "Bah." It was no one's business. Besides, she had always admired Madame Brunet as one of the dozen or so women in town who ran a business inherited from her deceased husband. They should be united, not at odds with one another.

"I'll send Claude to fetch these this afternoon," she said instead, nodding to the bread.

"He's growing, that youngster of yours."

At that, Marie smiled. "Seven years old and he thinks he's a man."

"Well, he is, yes? The man around the house. At least for now, eh?" One eyebrow bounced up in a question.

Marie swung to leave and almost collided with another woman who was also delivering her dough.

"Ah, Madame Jubert. Did you know the *Conqu*—?"

"Yes!" Marie interrupted. She slid past the newcomer and hurried out and down the stairs. This town! Did they have nothing better to do than speculate about her love life? Oh, if they only knew the truth about the Widow Jubert, maybe then they'd have something real to gossip about.

No doubt Capitaine de Monluc would be arriving through the Frederic Gate, the most impressive on the waterfront with a graceful arch and towering roof. Part of Marie wanted to avoid the man, to sneak around the corner and make her way to the Dauphin Gate by way of Rue Royale. On the other hand, she burned to know what was going on with her schooner. She'd have to ask Jerome in some kind of backhanded way.

"Paulette," she called to the girl, who still leaned over the sea wall, looking toward the harbor. "Walk with me, please?"

A cow dragged a cartload of turnips past, leaving in its wake an aroma of sweating animal and rotting vegetables. Paulette wrinkled her nose as she scurried over.

"I don't want to go down to the fishing shacks. I'm wearing my good shoes." She lifted her petticoat to expose delicate leather slippers. "Besides, it smells down there."

"You're always complaining about being bored, yet you won't do anything."

"Where are we going?"

"To meet Jerome."

Paulette skidded to a stop. "Marie?"

"I need to talk to him."

"Why do . . . ?" Her eyes widened. "Oh. The *Donna Rae*?"

"Keep your voice down. I want you to ask him about it." To many, Paulette appeared a spoiled, foolish girl, but Marie saw beneath the layers of frivolity and knew she could trust her.

"Me?"

"I can't very well, can I?"

"What excuse will I use?"

"You don't need an excuse. Just flirt with him a bit."

"He just thinks I'm a silly little girl."

"Exactly."

"Marie." She pouted.

"He's such a fool he *thinks* you're one," Marie clarified.

They stopped at the wide entrance to the Frederic Gate. Down the ramp, Capitaine de Monluc had just climbed out of the tender. He assumed a pose: one hand on a hip to push aside his pale coat, exposing the gold braid on his waistcoat, and his leg turned so the calf muscle bulged under his blue hose. He was a handsome man in his mid-forties, tall, with narrow shoulders that he compensated for with pads in his gray-white uniform coat. He habitually wore a black wig with short sides that curled over his ears, the long back tied with a ribbon. Years at sea had given him a ruddy complexion. His eyes were small and often bloodshot. At that moment they fixed on Marie and he smiled in a way that had her stomach knotting with anxiety.

Did he already know about the smuggling? Was there something on the *Donna Rae* to implicate her?

Chapter Two

When de Monluc saw Marie waiting for him at the gate, he paused to enjoy the moment. Her presence proved what he already believed: her disdain for him was all an act. He would conquer her one way or another. He positioned his tricorne on his head, straightened his back, and sauntered up the wharf. She looked delicious, tall and slender but with curves in the right places. He could see only a bit of her hair in the front as she kept her white cap pulled low on her forehead. The back gathered in a complicated coiffeur, but he imagined untying the thing and wrapping the auburn locks around his fist.

"Madame Jubert, Marie, what a pleasant surprise."

"Capitaine de Monluc," she said with a nod.

She looked nervous, although it might have been the chilly spring air making her draw the edges of her cloak together. Jerome preferred to think that his presence made her nervous.

"You know Mademoiselle Paulette Maigny," Marie said.

"Mademoiselle," Jerome said with a tilt of his head. "How are your parents?"

The girl had developed into a beautiful woman. She'd bring a hefty dowry to a marriage, and her parents had influence. If he hadn't already set his sights on Marie, he might have considered her for himself. There were five or six times more men in Louisbourg than women, so one such as her would be much in demand. No matter. Jerome intended to marry Marie-Charlotte Jubert, a woman of real property. She might dress like a working-class fishwife, but only out of thrift. He approved of that, for the time being. Once they were married she would have to choose attire more befitting his position.

"How was your trip, Capitaine?" Paulette said.

"Very successful." He glanced back down the gangway to the tender that had brought him ashore. "Yes, heads are going to roll."

Paulette batted her eyelashes. "Oh, my."

"In fact, I'm on my way to report directly to the governor."

"Do tell?" Paulette put her little hand on his forearm.

"I think the governor would like to be the first one told, don't you agree?"

"Oh, Capitaine, you must not keep us in suspense."

The little vixen was flirting with him. A glance at Marie had his smile broadening. She looked ready to choke something—so aggravated, in fact, a muscle jumped in the smooth curve of her jaw. He considered how to capitalize on this situation.

"What do they have down there?" Marie asked, motioning toward the sailors from the *Conquerant*, who unloaded crates from the tender onto the wharf.

"Contraband."

"Excuse me?"

She looked so startled that Jerome chuckled. He loved impressing the ladies. "I'm taking that lot up to the governor. It's proof of a smuggling operation I've discovered. And see there? That's my men bringing in the prisoners."

The sailors manned the oars of the two broad barges with practiced ease; each synchronized pull jolted the timbers and shoved them forward toward an opening in the sea wall, the main landing, marked by the elaborate arch in the shape of an oxen yoke standing on end. Matthew was crammed on a bench in the rear of the boat with two other men from the *Donna Rae*, Tom Smith on one side and Captain Gabe Martin on the other. The rest of the English crew occupied benches in the front. More were crammed in another boat keeping pace alongside.

Lynn M. Turner

How would the other men be treated? Would they have to stay in a dungeon all the time? Would there be enough food? How long until they could be exchanged for French prisoners? Months? Years? Ever?

As he swayed back and forth, Matthew forced himself to tamp down his anxiety and study the sea wall from this approach. He knew wood girded the stones to keep the salt water from eroding the mortar that held them together, but the planks had rotted to jagged ends at the high-water mark. It wouldn't take much to blow the thing to smithereens. On the other hand, if British ships made it into the harbor proper, it would be pretty much over for Louisbourg anyway, sea wall or no sea wall.

"That's the Widow Jubert, isn't it?" one of the French guards asked a man at the oars.

"That's her, yes," the other answered in a thick Parisian accent.

Matthew, who spoke both French and English fluently, was curious to see the person who would make two rough sailors sound so reverent. He turned to watch the widow glide down the wharf. He couldn't see her face from this angle, but she moved gracefully, tall and slender with square shoulders and a straight back. The sailors continued talking in French.

"And the other one?"

"Paulette Maigny."

"She's pretty."

"Doesn't hold a candle to the widow though, eh?"

"Watch your tongue, Pierre, that widow woman, she's promised to de Monluc, you know."

The captain of the *Donna Rae*, Gabe Martin, made a disgruntled sound under his breath, one that Matthew both heard and felt, as they were crushed against one another in the rocking tender. Although Matthew hadn't crewed on the *Donna Rae* for very long, he believed Martin sailed well and treated his men justly. The loss of his schooner and her cargo must have been hard to stomach. But at the moment Captain Martin looked not at the confiscated goods, but rather at the Widow Jubert.

The longboat knocked against the bumper of the wharf and a second later Matthew grabbed his knapsack, draped it over his right shoulder, and set foot on Louisbourg. He sniffed at the air: fresh and clean for the most part, but with subtle whiffs of coal fires, marsh water, and fish guts. Even here, on the lee side of the island, an ocean breeze kept the air moving.

The young widow reached the end of the wharf and walked right up to Matthew, but her attention was directed at the pile of crates near his leg. She shoved one of the boxes around to expose the owner's mark on the side. All color drained from her face. Thinking she might faint, Matthew took a step toward her. She glanced up, her brown eyes wide and frightened. In that instant, something jolted in his chest, driving the breath from him. Before he had a chance to open his mouth, she recovered. The transformation was so complete, from an expression of terror to one of indifference, he wondered if he'd imagined it all. After all, no one else seemed to notice.

He watched her swing around and hurry back up the wharf. His heart pounded as if he'd just had a terrible—or wonderful—shock. Then the widow stopped beside Capitaine de Monluc, the detestable man who commanded the frigate that had brought the *Donna Rae* in. The way she smiled at de Monluc had Matthew's jaw clenching. She was probably congratulating him on the seizure.

"All right, you swine," the French guard snapped near Matthew. "Form a line starting here."

Matthew winced when another soldier grabbed his arms and yanked them behind his back to wind his wrists with coarse hemp. He knew he had to act subserviently, so he curled his shoulders and stooped. He knew to remain silent and follow instructions. He knew to expect rough treatment, but he hadn't expected to hate the helplessness of it all so much. He twisted around to look at the widow woman again and was relieved to see she'd turned and was moving away.

Marie felt ill as she walked stiffly back along the quay and down the short Rue du Porte toward her own house. She heard one of her neighbors call a greeting, but the moment to return it had passed by the time the words registered. She felt stunned and frightened and bitterly regretful. Her beautiful schooner in de Monluc's clutches. Almost everything she had was tied in to the

Donna Rae. She'd lost it all: money, capital, investors, partners. She would have to start all over. Suddenly she had another, more horrifying thought. What if the authorities discovered her involvement? She'd be . . . what? Hanged? Certainly deported. And her babies!

She staggered to a corner, pulled her crucifix from under her bib, and clutched it. *Please, please, Blessed Mother, don't let anything hurt my children.*

When her dizziness passed, Marie continued along the street. She had to think clearly about this. What were the chances that she'd be caught? Who knew of her involvement? Only a couple of trusted people here in Louisbourg.

That man down on the wharf? He saw her react to the stamp on the *Donna Rae*'s cargo boxes. He had stepped forward when she faltered, so she felt certain he saw everything. She could picture him easily: tall, crystal blue eyes, dark hair and brows, wearing seaman's clothing. A couple of days' worth of whiskers gave his face a dark, dangerous look, but the concern in his eyes contradicted that. Would he mention it to anyone? He looked like a prisoner, so perhaps not. She hoped the crew of the *Donna Rae* knew better than to volunteer anything about the smuggling.

Marie and her children lived in a piquet cottage with a steep roof that flared out at the bottom like a bell and had gables on the front and back. Walls divided the ground floor into three rooms: a large kitchen, a tiny parlor, and, opening onto the street, a shop. The cottage abutted her large warehouse. She could hear voices through the door that opened into the shop.

Marie couldn't face anyone, so she pushed through the gate and stumbled along the side of the house and into the garden at the back. Here in the privacy of her own garden she sank down on a bench and let her face drop into her hands. Her breath heaved, as if she'd run all the way from the fishing property.

"Mama?"

"I didn't see you there, my little one," Marie said with a gasp. Her son knelt on a straw-lined path in the vegetable patch.

Claude looked wide-eyed. "You're crying."

"No, no, it's nothing." Her cheeks were wet, so she rubbed her apron firmly across her face. "What are you doing out here, anyway?"

He drew himself up straight and arranged an offended expression. "You told me to weed." He wore light pants that buttoned below his knees and a long tan vest. His hose drooped in folds around his shoes. His eyes were brown, like hers, and his face soft and smooth, still pale from the long winter.

Marie hated to see him struggling to be grown up. He'd turned seven a couple of months earlier, an important birthday because it marked the day he changed from his dresses of babyhood to the trousers and shirts like those worn by grown men. Marie felt so desolate, she wished she could pull him on her lap and hug him, but Claude thought himself beyond babying.

"Oh yes, so I did."

She looked down at the young pea vines emerging in the nearest raised bed, at the succulent green life. Logs standing on end enclosed the garden, protecting it from marauding livestock and humans. Here, sheltered from the ocean wind, black flies milled about. A goat bleated somewhere nearby, then a rooster crowed. Generally the garden calmed her. It was one of the few spots where she felt content, where she could work amid beauty and forget her worries. Not today.

"Didn't you go to the fishing station?" Claude asked.

"Something came up. I have to talk to Quentin." She pushed herself to a stand. "You go on with your weeding. You're doing a very good job."

As she entered the kitchen through the back door Marie shrugged off her cloak and hung it on a peg. Years earlier, when she was first married, her husband had indulged his child bride, allowing her to put some effort into making her new home pretty. She had cleaned the black off the beams and whitewashed the walls. She scrubbed the pretty sideboard and filled it with the china unearthed from trunks found under the eaves. It had all seemed like playing house then, at least during the daylight hours. By the time she'd turned sixteen, she was heavy with child and her elderly husband had all but lost interest in her.

Because it was still early in the day, she expected to see the second child from that marriage playing at the table, but the room was empty. Marie leaned back out the door. "Claude, where is Fleurie?"

"*Grand-mère* took her out."

"Bah." Marie didn't like her daughter spending so much time with her grandmother; the woman spoiled her and put unrealistic ideas into her head. But it hardly seemed important at that moment. After all, if the worst happened, Marie's mother could take custody of Fleurie for good. She took a quivering breath and went into the front room where Quentin Bauldry, her foreman, dealt with a customer.

Quentin was an easygoing, middle-aged man who carried his bulky body over the peninsula each morning to work in Marie's business, and then returned to his family at night. When Marie counted her blessings, she always placed him at the top of her list. He was such a good and loyal man.

"You're back early," he said, frowning at her.

She made a noncommittal sound and nodded at the customer, a stranger, thankfully, who didn't expect her to make small talk. While Quentin finished measuring out the cordage and rolling it in a tight loop between his elbow and shoulder, Marie tidied up by replacing tops on barrels and neatly piling some anchor baskets. Finally the customer left and Quentin looked at her.

"What's wrong? You're as white as your apron."

"The *Donna Rae* has been impounded."

He sat heavily on a canvas bale. "Are you sure?"

"I saw her with my own eyes."

"Saints preserve us. Do they know what she carried?"

"Jerome de Monluc took her for smuggling."

He groaned. "De Monluc. The louse."

"I don't know what went wrong, Quentin. No one's ever interfered with the trade before."

He turned his eyes heavenward. "Thank the good Lord you had the sense to keep your involvement secret."

"I mortgaged everything for this."

He looked pained and sat staring into space for a moment. "We'll have to stop giving the fishermen advances. Call in some loans."

A pain throbbed in her forehead. "It's four more months until the season ends."

This time of year, Marie's warehouse advanced everything the offshore fishermen might need for the season: canvas, extra sail, anchors, cables, salt pork, biscuits. . . . Then, when the season ended, she received payment, often in the form of dried cod, which she then added to her own stock and shipped the lot out to Europe. Meanwhile, she had to keep her inshore fishermen and shore workers fed and supplied. It was a fine balancing act, one that she thought she had mastered. That's why she had gambled on this big shipment.

"Why, oh why, was I so greedy?" she wailed.

"It seemed like such a sure thing." Quentin suddenly looked hopeful. "Maybe they didn't get a chance to take on the cargo?"

Marie shook her head. "She's riding low."

"Gabe Martin knows his business. He could have her full of ballast or something?"

"No, I saw our partners' mark on the crates."

"You got close enough to see them?" he asked, alarmed.

"I had to know what happened so I met Jerome at the gate. I know, I know," she said at his look of distaste. "Paulette and I. There was a man, Quentin. I think he was a crew member from the schooner. He saw me look at the crate."

Once again she saw the man in her mind's eye, his eyes especially, large and blue and intelligent. Where Jerome de Monluc was handsome in a refined, almost pretty way, the man on the dock had uneven features that should have been disagreeable but weren't. Marie pressed the flat of her hand on her stomach. How could she have been thinking about that man's face at a time like this?

"A man from the *Donna Rae*?" Quentin asked.

"I think so."

"Then he's not likely to give you away. There's nothing around here about the schooner, is there?" Quentin asked.

"Only the bills of exchange. They're safely locked in the warehouse."

"Do you think you should destroy them?"

"Not yet. There might be some hope left. What if the

Donna Rae is suddenly released? Or sneaks out of the harbor? If I don't have those credit slips, I won't be able to take payment. I'll wait and see what happens. Meanwhile, we'll have to find money somewhere."

"The crew," Quentin said with a shake of his head. "I'm sorry for them."

"I am as well. They'll be put to work around the town, yes?" When Quentin nodded, she continued, "We'll take on that man, the one who saw me."

"Why? Did he look suspicious?"

She shrugged. "I don't know. Maybe. I'm so confused. Why did they take the *Donna Rae*? She's just one of hundreds of schooners in these waters, lots of them doing what we were."

"Anyone else caught?"

"I don't know." She marched back and forth across the room, going six paces each way. "I wanted to ask, but I was afraid of looking too interested."

"We'll find out soon enough. It'll be all over town before night." There were 4,500 permanent citizens in Louisbourg, and thousands of migratory workers, and every one of them wanted to know everyone else's business.

Quentin happened to be facing the open door. "Here comes your brother."

Marie stopped her pacing. "How to make a bad day worse." She wrapped her arms around her midsection and waited.

At twenty-six, Bernard Bretel was two years older than Marie. He was short and thin and always smelled of spruce beer. She wished he acted like a doting brother, someone who felt sorry for her young widowhood, someone who worried and fretted about the stress she endured raising her two children alone. Bah. Bernard felt none of those sentiments. Instead he envied and resented her.

"Sister," Bernard said as soon as he stepped in the door.

"Why aren't you down at the shore?" she demanded. She'd learned from long experience that it was always best to go on the offensive with her brother.

"I could say the same thing about you."

"I don't manage that property, Bernard, you do. I own it. So why are you here? Is something wrong?"

Ignoring her, he scuffed across the room and picked up a line weight. "I heard something just now." He tossed the weight up into the air on the end of his fingers.

She flicked an alarmed look at Quentin: could Bernard know about the *Donna Rae?* "I asked you a question, Bernard."

"You know Jerome de Monluc is back."

She pretended to misunderstand him. "Bah! Why does everyone ask me that?"

Now Bernard looked her straight in the eye. The malicious glint she saw there struck her like a blow. Why did he hate her so much? He was her brother.

Was it because he knew about the *Donna Rae*? About her involvement? She felt the color rising up her neck and that infuriated her. Any weakness on her part would only make him happy.

Quentin asked through the tension, "What did you hear, Bernard?"

"That Marie was waiting for de Monluc when he landed, for one thing."

She scoffed. "Paulette wanted to talk to him, if it's any of your business."

"And you came rushing back here like you were crying or something."

Marie sniffed as if disinterested but her mind raced. Someone must have seen her. Someone who went running to Bernard. "Is that why you're here? To gloat about some gossip you heard? I'm sorry to disappoint you, brother, but as you can see, I'm fine. Now I suggest you get back to work while you still have a job to get back to."

"What's that supposed to mean?"

"It means just what I said. If you won't do your job, I'll find someone who will." Her heart thudded in her throat but she fought to keep her tone and expression neutral.

"You wouldn't dare. What would people say if you fired your own brother, eh?"

"They'd say, 'About time.' "

Bernard spat out a derogatory curse.

Quentin stood. "Bernard!"

"You keep out of this, old man."

Marie stepped between the two men and stared up at her brother. "I mean it, Bernard. I warned you last time. I won't allow you to run my business into the ground. Now get back to work or you're fired."

"We'll see about that," Bernard snapped as he stomped out of the building.

Chapter Three

The Rue Toulouse began at the quay directly across from the Frederic Gate and sloped upward. It was a wide street with tall stone buildings on either side, many decorated with fleurs de lys. Matthew watched his feet to avoid the wheel ruts and crevices where water had gouged long ribbons in the dirt. The leather strap of his knapsack slipped down to his elbow but he couldn't adjust it with his hands tied behind his back, so he dragged its canvas behind him. He felt embarrassed and exposed, as if he were walking naked.

People appeared in the windows and stepped from buildings to stand on sidelines and stare at the eight English prisoners. They had good reason to hate New Englanders; it had only been six years since the southern colonists marched on the fortress and besieged it, causing horrible weeks of terrifying bombardment, weeks of death and deprivation culminating in a humiliating surrender. Most of the people now living in Louisbourg had been present during that siege. They had personal tragedies, their own nightmares, and their own grudges. The treaty at the war's end had returned the Isle Royale to France, but that, Matthew had assumed, would do little for the bitter memories.

Now he wondered. A few poisonous glares came their way, but most of the people seemed more curious and amused at the sight of English prisoners being led like cattle up the hill. When a scrawny man tossed a clump of horse droppings at Captain Martin, the crowd laughed but they didn't pick up their own missiles. The captain kept his eyes rigidly forward.

After half a dozen blocks, the prisoner procession neared a massive citadel. Here the ground leveled out and soldiers drilled lethargically around the parade square. Their white coats were soiled and worn, the wool in places as dark as the blue facings showing on the inside of the coattails. Nearby a young lad in bright red and blue thumped a rhythm on his drum.

The King's Bastion hunkered at the top of the peninsula, a long building with a dozen chimneys and two tiers of perhaps three dozen windows along the front, not including the smaller gables in the slate roof. A clock tower rose above the center entrance. The prisoners and their guards passed through an outer gate and stumbled to a standstill next to a guardhouse while the soldiers conferred.

Matthew's heart thudded. He knew what to expect. He had good reason to believe that everything would be all right in the end. And yet, standing there, dwarfed below the imposing walls, his mouth grew parched with fear. He took a few sidesteps to look down into a trench about fifteen feet below the drawbridge. Verdant grass blanketed the sides, and a narrow ditch of stagnant water wallowed at the bottom.

"You studying the fort?" Tom Smith whispered.

Matthew jerked around. "Pardon?"

"You're planning to escape, ain't ya?" Tom had bushy eyebrows over small eyes, spaced close together over a thin nose with a prominent ridge. At the moment, they were wide and expectant.

"Escape?" Matthew almost laughed. "And go where?"

"Ya get a boat," Tom snapped, insulted. "Ya go down to the mainland."

"That's possible, of course," Matthew said, regretting his sarcastic tone, "but I'm thinking I'll just wait it out. We'll get ransomed."

"You believe that, do ya? Ya figure the likes of us are worth something?"

"But of course. The owners—"

"All they care about is their money. There's no money for them in ransoming us."

Soon the prisoners were led into a small room where

wide wooden benches sat in two tiers along the walls and straw covered the floor. Light fell in through a barred window. Not the dark, mildewed room that Matthew had feared, but a prison nonetheless.

Over the next twenty hours the prisoners were fed ample amounts of bread and dried meat and allowed to go in ones and twos to the same latrine that the soldiers used. They were used to tight quarters on the schooner, the curved buttocks of the man swinging above them, snorts and snores, the timbers creaking. But the sounds here were different—quieter, more furtive, harder to sleep through.

The next morning, they shuffled out into the open courtyard of the bastion. Apparently word had gone out around the town that there were prisoners available for work. The potential employers milled about the New Englanders, looking them over like slaves at a market as they stood in a ragged line scratching their lice bites and squinting in the sun.

Here in the fortress, where soldiers worked like ants on a hill, the woman's skirts looked out of place. Although she wore a wide bonnet that cast a shadow on her face and had her shawl wrapped tightly about her upper body, Matthew recognized her immediately. He shuffled sideways to look beyond the men blocking his view. She lifted her chin and looked him straight in the eye. He felt the eye contact like a fist slamming into his chest. Something about the way her body stiffened made him believe she felt the same connection flowing between them. He started to straighten, caught himself, and returned to his submissive slouch.

Marie nodded at Matthew, said something to the man beside her, turned, and walked off toward a tunnel through the rampart. Matthew watched her disappear through the stone arch. That feeling he got when he looked at her, that physical reaction, was strange and worrying. Probably just something to do with the circumstances. He turned to listen to the discussion going on before him.

The French translator was short and slender. He wore a clean, brushed uniform, the leathers freshly dyed. He seemed to take his duties seriously.

Captain Martin asked the translator, "What steps have been taken to inform the *Donna Rae*'s owners of our situation?"

"Someone is working on that at this very moment. We're a very organized people."

"You'll keep me informed?"

"Naturally."

"Will we be charged and put on trial?"

"That is up to Governor Desherbier's discretion, but he may prefer to sanction your actions with a punishment that will deter future offenses."

The captain paused to take that in. He asked, "Will I get the *Donna Rae* back?"

"Your vessel may be ransomed as well, but I doubt it.

It will likely be confiscated. Since your kind took our fishing boats during your . . . er . . . occupation, we are short of them."

"I'd like to meet with your commanding officer."

"That can be arranged, Captain, but as you are a civilian, I expect he will defer to one of the governor's representatives."

The soldier looked up and down the line of prisoners and raised his voice. "My clerk has a list of the work you will be doing." He nodded to a man who carried a rolled document.

"Do we get a choice?"

"Naturally. If some of you are, for example, experienced with stone and mortar, you will be sent to work on the battlement repair."

Matthew raised his eyebrows. They'd let the enemy work on their own defensive walls? He wished he had some experience in that area so he could scramble around the ramparts and study the terrain outside the walls.

"You're not here as our guests," the soldier continued, "You will work for your food and lodging. If you follow our rules, you'll eventually get more freedom. Prove yourselves valuable and your employer might give you a bonus. You can buy things with that, perhaps drink or a meal."

"Will my men be billeted about town?" Captain Martin asked.

"In time."

The men muttered in relief. The dungeon was cold, damp, and crowded. Even though the straw brought in was fairly fresh, it crawled with vermin.

"Will we be free to move about town?" Captain Martin asked.

"In a limited way. It's up to your employer. If any of you make an obvious attempt to escape, we will shoot you. And you are required to abide by our laws. Any infraction by one prisoner will be punished by everyone."

The captain's voice rose. "What do you mean?"

"If one of you breaks our laws or tries to escape, all of you will receive the punishment."

"What kind of punishment?"

"It depends on the infraction, naturally."

"That hardly seems fair."

"For swearing or blaspheming the name of God, the Blessed Virgin, or the saints, you will have your tongue pierced by a hot iron."

"But sir, my men are not Gallican Catholic. Their habits—"

"Are of no concern! You are on French soil and will respect our ways!"

Matthew glanced over at Tom Smith. The man had a nasty habit of cursing, taking the Lord's name in vain. He did it by rote, not with a malicious intent, but that wouldn't matter to the people of Louisbourg. The first chance he had, Matthew decided, he'd drill some non-blasphemous words into Tom's head to try to break him of the habit. Even so, they would all be living in fear of having a hot iron poked through their tongues.

There were probably other laws uniquely French that these New Englanders would not be schooled in. What were the punishments for those infractions? Why, they could be put to death for something that they did by habit in New England. He looked around at the tanned faces. Old and young, angry or frightened, they were good men. They didn't deserve this.

At that moment the magnitude of what he'd done slammed Matthew like a log between the eyes. He longed to call it all off, to change his mind, to go back a few months and say no, *I won't do it!* What had seemed like a simple job, an adventure for a worthy cause, suddenly took on a horrific countenance. An acid regret gnawed in his belly. Still, he gritted his teeth and lowered his eyes while the soldiers divvied up the available work. His background was not in manual labor, but he couldn't very well tell them about his real trade, not yet, not until his contact arrived. Everyone thought him a ship's hand and, at this point, it seemed safer to keep it that way. The fact that he spoke both French and English fluently should have, he thought, garnered him a soft job, maybe as a clerk. Not so. The prisoners of Louisbourg were expected to perform the most menial of duties. That's why Matthew, accompanied by his new employer, headed to a fishing property just outside the fortress walls.

*   *   *

"What's your name?"

"Matthew Carter. And yours?"

"Jean Riverin. I'm the shoremaster."

"As I said back there, I know nothing about curing fish," Matthew warned.

"We'll teach you. Your part won't be complicated." He paused, pointing ahead. "This is Rue Petit Etang. Watch for this lime kiln when you come back and you shouldn't have any trouble finding your way."

Jean had spoken in a friendly voice, as if Matthew were a regular inhabitant of the town and not a prisoner. Matthew took a moment to study him and, judging by his accent and clothing, decided Jean was Basque, from the southwest corner of France. Everything about him spoke of fish, the salt stains curling around his legs, the white, cracked skin on his hands, and the pervasive stink of fish guts about his being.

"Will I return after dark?"

Jean nodded. "There will be lanterns on the corners. And this is the Dauphin Gate."

Matthew looked up at the battlements then down upon a marshy sluiceway below. There were two guards on either end of the bridge spanning the water. Both watched them approaching.

"How is it you, a Frenchman, were with those English?" Jean asked.

"I live in the New Hampshire Grant."

"But you are obviously French?"

"My mother is from France, my father from England."

"You don't talk like a seaman either."

Matthew smiled. "Town living."

When they passed through the second gate without being hailed by a guard, Matthew asked, "Will I have any trouble getting back into town?"

Jean shook his head. "They'll know who you are, yes? It's their job."

They walked for five more minutes around a curve of beach crowded with split fish drying on every available surface: rocks, gravel, tables made of twigs, even on the roofs of the shingled buildings. The landward side of the peninsula stretched for miles, treeless except for wind-twisted scrub. It had probably been thick forest at one time, but the townspeople had cut the wood for heat.

Matthew turned to look back at the fortress. It would be difficult for the enemy to approach from this side; those manning the battlements would have a clear shot for a wide arc.

Here and there men moved along the lines of fish, turning them over one after the other. A woman in a striped skirt chopped at the ground in a tiny fenced garden. Two little boys scurried around her, their childhood skirts caked with grime. Such an innocent scene. It made him smile.

The docks along the shore here were much less substantial than those that adjoined the fortress proper, just stages built to go right into the sea. The wood rising above the high-water mark was white with seagull droppings.

"The shallops will be back in another hour or so," Jean explained. "Then we'll get busy. At this time of day, you will do the same as those fellows, turning the fish. If there's any sign of rain, we get them under cover quickly, you understand. Day or night."

Ahead of them, a man strode out from between two shacks. He stared at Matthew with belligerent, rheumy eyes. Like Jean, he wore a white linen shirt, dark woolen trousers, and wooden shoes. "Took you long enough. Is this him?"

Jean nodded. "Matthew, this is—"

"He experienced?"

"No, Bernard, but—"

"Why didn't you get someone experienced?"

"But . . ." Jean hesitated and pursed his lips. Finally he said briskly, "He speaks French. I was lucky to get him. The others went to repair the walls."

"Bah, repairs. If it weren't for his sort, we wouldn't need repairs. Bloody English."

"I am French," Matthew said softly. This coarse, thin man had his hackles rising.

Bernard stared at him a moment, then, in an obvious dismissal, turned back to Jean. "Get him started right away."

"All right. I'll just fetch him an apron."

"He doesn't need one." He turned on his heel and strode off toward the town, his shoulders back, chest out like a scrawny rooster.

"Who was that?"

"Bernard Bretel. He's a kind of manager. I am the shoremaster on this station." When Matthew gave him a blank look, Jean continued, "That means that I oversee the operation on shore. Bernard, well, he . . . he just oversees me, I suppose." He looked disgruntled.

"He owns the station?"

"No, his sister does."

Ah, his sister. The Widow Jubert? He didn't want to be obvious, so he asked about the brother first. "Does he manage other stations as well as this one?"

"Why should you care? Here we are, the Jubert station."

"The Widow Jubert's?"

Jean frowned suspiciously. "You know of her?"

"The soldiers bringing me to shore pointed her out." He looked around, smiling, hoping to see her.

Jean grabbed Matthew's forearm and pinched hard. "You keep clear of her."

Other than yanking his arm free, Matthew didn't respond. He was a prisoner now, a shoreworker, the *garçon*. He followed Jean silently.

"We keep the salt and the aprons in here." Jean said, leaning through the door to a small structure built of branches standing on end and tied with rope. Grass sprouted from the roof. Jean emerged with two crusted leather aprons and threw one to Matthew. It wrapped around the midriff with a pointed bib that tied with a thong around the neck.

"We have two shallops. They'll throw the cod onto

the stage and you'll haul it in buckets back to the split-ter. He'll dress them." Jean spoke as he walked toward the lapping water. "The head goes in this bucket, the liver in here, the scrap on the ground, and the rest onto that table."

He pointed to a waist-high counter that had two boards nailed on its surface and a long, narrow knife standing in a holder. The ground under the table, lush green grass and clumps of rotted flesh, hummed with fat flies. Ugh, the smell. Matthew hoped he would learn to breathe through his mouth.

"You'll wash the fish in this." Jean looked into a wooden box lined in a dark tar-like material. "This should have been filled by now. Grab a bucket."

Salt and fish scales coated everything. He and Jean sloshed back and forth down to the water. They filled two leather buckets on each trip and poured them into the cleaning box. As they worked, Jean continued with his lecture.

"Once they're cleaned, take them to the salter over there. He'll be sending you into the shed for more salt now and again. You run when someone tells you to do something, eh?"

"Is there only one splitter?" Jean nodded. Matthew couldn't see how he'd have to run anywhere if every-one else had to wait for the splitter to finish with each fish.

Jean smiled as if reading his mind. "You'll see. He can work fast, that one. Been doing it all his life. When the salter's done with them, you lay them out on the flakes over there. You understand?"

"Yes," Matthew said with a shrug. "The fish get unloaded from the boats and I carry them up to the splitter. He cleans them and then I take the fish to the salter. He salts them and I carry them over to those twig tables. A very simple procedure."

"No, not so simple," Jean corrected. "It's very complicated. These are skilled workers. Madame Jubert was very lucky to get them."

Matthew thought about the leathery, white pieces of dried fish he'd seen all his life. He personally had never cooked it, as that was the job of his mother or her cook. "But I thought dried cod is all the same?"

"No, not the same. The fish must be perfect to bring the best price. Prepared while it is still fresh, salted just right."

"How will I know if I put too much—"

"You! You won't have anything to do with it. You are the boy, nothing more. Maybe someday. . . ." He heaved a Gallic shrug.

"Well then, what happens if someone puts on too much salt?"

"It burns the fish so it breaks. Not enough salt and it turns red when it dries."

Matthew made a mental note to study the fish the next time he was in a market. Ah, the market. He never thought he would feel a fondness for the place, but at this moment he even missed that noisy, dirty square near his home. The markets he'd recently seen in New England bore little resemblance to the ones he'd known all his life. In this place, at this time, there wasn't a soul with whom he could even talk about home—his real home.

"Finish filling the wash tank, then top up the salt barrel. If I'm not back by then, go help the boy over there turn the fish. I'm going to buy the mackerel and herring for tomorrow's bait." He turned on his heel and strode up the bank.

And suddenly Matthew was alone. He felt a bit stunned at first. For one thing, he'd spent the previous weeks crowded on the schooner, bumping into someone every time he moved. For another thing, he hadn't imagined he would be left alone, especially outside the fortress walls. He looked up the shore where skiffs were pulled up on the gravel. If he wanted, he could jog over there, grab a boat, push off, and head . . . where? He wouldn't get far before someone noticed that wasn't his skiff. They'd be able to run by land around to the harbor narrows much faster than he could row there himself. It would simply be a matter of heading him off, or shooting him like a bird on a rock.

He could, if he really wanted to escape, hoof it over the peat behind him and head inland, to perhaps spend a few weeks traveling until he found a settlement. It would be rugged going. He'd likely sink in mud holes and trip on branches the whole time. Slow going. And the soldiers on the ramparts could use him as target practice. Luckily, he thought, he didn't want to escape.

He grabbed two buckets and walked down to the plank staging that served as a dock. Seaweed undulated just under the surface of the water and a starfish clung to a barnacle-encrusted rock. White bubbles outlined the edge of the highest point where each little wave washed ashore. He watched a moment, thinking that the tide was coming in.

Here and there the breeze snatched white crests from the top of the water. To the right, slate roofs glimmered over the tops of the fortress walls. White smoke rising from the chimneys drifted like skeins of wool from east to west. The sky was a luminescent blue here, quite different from home. He hadn't expected Louisbourg to be so attractive. As the wind came off the water, he pushed back his shoulders and took a huge, cleansing breath. He'd been breathing in shallow, tense puffs for so long, he'd forgotten what it felt like to really fill his lungs. He lifted his arms high over his head and stretched his fingers wide.

"What are you doing?" a woman's voice asked.

Matthew swung around and gaped at Marie-Charlotte Jubert. His first thought was that no one that precious should be standing near fish offal. Her clothes were a practical coarse weave and she wore no adornments at all, not even a ruffle at her elbow, and yet she seemed like a lady. He sighed at her impossibly soft-looking skin and the long, graceful line of her neck as if he'd never seen a woman before. Somewhere in the back of his mind he knew he was being rude, but he couldn't seem to stop himself.

Suddenly Marie drew herself up and stared him in the eye. "Well? What is it?"

"Madame?"

"You obviously have something to say to me. You may as well get it over with."

"We've never even met, Madame." Somewhere in the recesses of his mind he knew that it was pride that kept him standing tall and staring her straight in the eye, when he should have been scuffing his feet and looking at the ground.

"I know who you are." She shifted the heavy basket to her other forearm.

"You . . . know who I am?" Who he really was? How could this be? He stepped to look beyond her, up to the buildings, expecting to see soldiers. But other than the couple of men working the fish further up the beach, they were alone. He calmed down. "Tell me who you think I am."

Chapter Four

"You're a prisoner from the *Donna Rae.*" Marie's pulse thudded in her throat.

The man took a deep breath, as if to release the tension in his shoulders. "You are remarkably knowledgeable about the names of the vessels in the harbor, Madame Jubert."

She stepped back. Something about him made her feel self-conscious. Perhaps it was the way he leaned forward slightly, as if he would at any moment spring upon her. He certainly looked strong enough to wrestle her to the ground. At that thought, her heart jumped, but not with fear. With . . . something else, something unfamiliar and unsettling. He had beautiful eyes, the color of a storm-tossed sea.

The fact that she kept thinking about his eyes unsettled Marie; she wasn't normally so sentimental. It was dangerous to be so. She said briskly, "Of course I know the vessel's name. Everyone is talking about the arrest."

She looked at him through narrowed eyes. His voice might sound like a fellow countryman, but he was loyal to the king of England, a French-speaking man willingly living on British soil. Marie willingly made money from them, but she would never forget what the men from New England had done to her and to her neighbors. Never.

On March 18, 1744, France had declared war on Britain. The news reached Louisbourg before it reached the English colonies, and they took advantage of this by attacking and capturing British Canso. But the war took a dreadful turn. In May 1745, while a British naval squadron blockaded the harbor, a New England fleet arrived in the bay, landed troops, and began a vicious bombardment. The weeks of the siege were a living hell.

She clutched at that memory to keep from thinking of this prisoner as a man.

She didn't know what to do with her hands, so she braced them on her hips and tried to look belligerent. She owned this property. He was a prisoner, a worker, not someone to cower before. She was only talking to him because she needed to know if he'd seen her shock at recognizing the symbol on the goods on the wharf. And if he had seen it, did he understand the implications? Would he blackmail her? Or give her away to the authorities?

He wore a loose-sleeved shirt, the brown color faded

at the shoulders, a long black vest, striped trousers, and wooden shoes. The same sort of thing other sailors wore. But on him, they looked different. Perhaps it was the confident way he carried himself, or how the muscles of his shoulders and legs moved under the time-softened fabric despite their loose fit. He was used to command, that one. She'd place a bet on it.

She risked another look at his compelling eyes and read no malice there. Nevertheless, she felt sure no prisoner would be so calm unless he had the advantage somehow. And how did he know her name? She snorted, trying to appear indifferent, and then felt embarrassed by the sound.

"Where is Bernard?" she snapped.

"He walked off."

No surprise there, she thought. "And Jean?"

"Gone to get bait."

"You know what you're to do?"

"Yes, Madame."

"Then get to it." She lifted her skirts and swung around.

"Madame."

The soft voice filled her with tension. "Yes?"

"As I am in your employ, you should know my name." He paused, but she said nothing. "It's Matthew Carter."

She turned the foreign-pronounced name over in her mind. He didn't look like a Matthew Carter. He looked like a highwayman, a leader of a gang, sure of himself, someone who enjoyed life and lived recklessly. Bah! The man made her feel like a blithering schoolgirl. She'd waste no more time on him.

Marie strode up the bank. Halfway to the cottage she looked back. Matthew was on his knees on the skid, dipping the bucket into the water.

The cottage was a small building with a thatched roof, dirt floor, and bare windows except when the shutters were pulled closed in storms. A cold, dank building, it was only used in the fishing season and contained the immediate necessities. The interior walls divided it into a large main room, with half a dozen long plank tables, and two smaller rooms. Jean Riverin used one of them as his private quarters, and the two shallop masters slept in the other.

"Good morning, Suzette," Marie said to the girl leaning over the table.

Suzette bobbed a half curtsy. This was her first season working for Marie and she still acted as if everything she said and did could spell the end of her career. "Good morning, Madame Jubert."

"I'm sorry I didn't come here yesterday. How did you make out?" She set the basket carefully on the dirt floor then revolved her aching shoulders to loosen the tight muscles.

"I fed them bread and cheese, Madame."

"Did they give you a hard time?"

Suzette mumbled, "Only a little."

Marie doubted that. The men expected, and deserved, a hearty meal to keep them sustained through the hard hours of the fishing season. She exchanged her apron for a more serviceable one. "We'll make it up to them today. I've brought ham, bacon, and goose thighs. Set the spider, please."

Suzette poked the wood around until she had a pile of red coals in the front center of the chin-high fireplace. Then, with her hands wrapped in old rags, she dragged the spider, a frying pan with legs and a long handle, over the searing heat.

Marie unloaded the basket onto the table and began to cut up the ham, bacon, and goose thighs into manageable portions. As she worked, she wondered how Matthew Carter knew her name. She'd met with Captain Martin a few weeks earlier, within sight of a couple of the schooner's crew members, in a secluded cove up the shore. It had been a clear, cold morning. She and Quentin had taken a small sailboat up, ostensibly to check on a new fishing station, but really to give Captain Martin instructions and money. The thought of that lost money made her groan aloud.

"Madame?" Suzette asked.

"Fetch some vegetables for the bisque." She pulled a narrow blade through the ham. Perhaps she shouldn't have brought such an expensive meal. It was likely that money would be scarce in the upcoming months, even if she did survive the loss of the schooner.

Soon the pieces of meat sizzled and spat in a great dollop of lard. While it browned, Marie and Suzette cut mounds of cabbage, onions, carrots, and parsnips, pausing occasionally to stir the meat. When the vegetables were ready, they poured a rich bouillon into the pan with the meat. Steam billowed. Then meat, vegetables, and more liquid all went into a heavy old kettle. It took both women to lift it onto the hook suspended on the crane.

Marie reached through the slit in her skirt for her pocket and dug out her *mignonette*, a bag of spices. She held the cheesecloth to her nose, drawing in the rich aroma of red pepper, cinnamon, nutmeg, and coriander, then she dropped it into the pot.

As the food cooked, Marie and Suzette set about their daily routine of scrubbing the planks on the table, airing out the feather mattresses, and sweeping the dirt floor. The physical work helped, but Marie still ruminated on her troubles.

When the hoarse cries of seagulls announced the arrival of the two shallops, Marie leaned her shoulder on the rough wood of the doorjamb, crossed her arms under her chest, and watched the approach. Their gunnels rode low over the water, a sign of a good morning. A moment later, the masters tacked for the last approach and the crew pulled down the gray sails as they drifted into the dock.

Marie watched as Matthew hurried with the other men down to the boats and reached to pull the first shallop up. He turned and smiled at the other *garçon*. Then it seemed that his eyes traveled past the boy and up to the door where Marie stood. She felt exposed there for an instant, caught in his eyes. Then he turned back to his work.

What would she do if the prisoner decided to try to buy his freedom by turning her over to the authorities? Would she run away? Impossible. She would never abandon her children. Her mother could look after them, she knew, but not well. Marie's own upbringing proved that fact. If only she knew what was going on. She would have to think of a way to get Matthew to carry a message to Captain Martin.

Matthew stood knee-deep in the water now, his thighs braced against the wood, and leaned into the shallop. When he emerged, he carried a codfish in his arms like a sleeping toddler. The other men laughed. Matthew, smiling sheepishly, thrashed back up the slippery stones and heaved the fish into a waist-high crate. The wet breeches molded to his legs, outlining the muscles. Jean Riverin slapped him on the back and handed him an iron hook. Matthew studied it a moment, then strode back into the water.

Marie had to admit that Matthew appeared to be taking the work with good cheer. He was a prisoner, yet he didn't look subservient or resentful; rather, he seemed keen to learn. Would she be so good-natured in his position? She doubted it. His legs had to be numb from the cold and soon his hands would sting with salt.

When she saw that the fish had all been tossed into the boxes on the skid and the shallops secured, Marie turned back to the fire, swung the kettle of bisque off and, with Suzette's help, lifted it off the hooks and onto the hearth where it would stay warm. She scooped out four servings, plopped them into a crock, and stuffed a cork in the opening. Those would be eaten at her own table that night. Then she fished the bag of spices out of the kettle and tossed it into the fire, where it sizzled a moment before sinking into the red coals.

The shoreworkers continued their labor out on the beach, but the shallops' masters and crew scuffed into the cottage, each of them greeting her politely. They tiredly pulled off their jackets and knit toques and hung them around the walls. Greasy hair, burnt noses, blackened fingernails—they were an uncouth-looking lot, but they worked hard and didn't cheat her. Marie set wooden platters of bread on the table while Suzette poured pitchers of spruce beer. The men fetched their own bowls and spoons from a sideboard and lined up before the pot.

With one last look around the room to see that everything had been done, Marie packed up her basket and hoisted it over her arm. By the time she was ready to step outside, the men had said grace and were hunched over their food, making appreciative smacking sounds with their lips.

Marie stepped outside and paused to watch the shoreworkers, Matthew in particular. Too bad, she mused, that all those good looks were wasted on an Englishman. Bah, she shouldn't be thinking like that. Men were no end of trouble, good-looking or not. She swung around to the path leading to the main track and left.

By now Matthew had been laboring with the fish a couple of hours and no longer noticed the smell. He and the other *garçon* had worked quickly, first dragging the ungainly fish, most as long as his leg and a sluggish flapping weight, onto the tables, and then through the stages to the final drying racks. His fingers stung from salt crusting and melting into new scrapes and cuts.

"We're getting low here," the salter said, indicating the dwindling mound of white grains on his table.

With a nod of acquiescence, Matthew grabbed the dry wooden buckets and started toward the building storing the salt. As he'd done every time, he glanced into the kitchen trying to see Marie and the girl as they moved about the fireplace. He was disappointed when she was nowhere in sight.

Why, he wondered as he scooped out salt from the barrel, did she do all that labor herself? Sure, she dressed like a simple cook, but according to the sailors the day before, she was a wealthy woman. He remembered that they'd said Capitaine de Monluc intended on marrying the widow woman. That proved she was rich. The pig of a capitaine didn't seem the type to marry someone without a hefty dowry. Surely the widow knew what sort of man de Monluc was? She wouldn't actually marry him, would she? A woman like her would have her choice of suitors. Everyone seemed to know her, even Captain Martin.

Matthew froze as suspicion crept up his spine like a venomous snake. He distinctly remembered the way Captain Martin reacted to those sailors when they were talking about Marie Jubert and how de Monluc meant to have her. He was furious. Captain Martin knew her, but how? Matthew closed his eyes and replayed the scene on the wharf the day before, the way Madame Jubert had almost swooned. Could she be the secret French owner of the *Donna Rae*? His eyes sprung open. She'd be ruined. Or worse. Jailed, deported.

"Oh, sweet Mary," he prayed, "please, please don't let her be the one."

And what if she was? He grabbed the buckets, his hands around the rope so hard the knuckles blanched white. Too late now to change the past, to languish under regret. Perhaps no one else in Louisbourg knew about her involvement. They wouldn't hear it from him. Even if she remained undiscovered, she had to have lost money on the venture—a lot of money. He wouldn't be able to make that up to her, not yet, but by the sweet Mary, he'd do all he could to protect her.

Chapter Five

Six days after arriving in the fortress, Matthew decided he knew all there was to know about being a shoreworker on a fishing property. He slopped the cleaned fillets into a bucket and hauled them along to the wooden flakes, then lined them up in flat and precise lines. When the day's catch was all prepared, he went back to earlier ones and turned them over. The fish got more leather-like with each visit.

The mindless work gave him plenty of time to think. He tried to concentrate on the town's layout, to draw imaginary maps and engineer drawings in his mind, editing them when he discovered something new on his walks to and from the prison. He chatted with the other shoreworkers and got friendly with Jean Riverin, the real master of this station. Those distractions occupied only moments of his waking day; thoughts of Marie Jubert filled the rest.

Was that a result of being lonely? Or bored? He was certainly both. He found himself watching for Marie's approach, waiting, timing his trips to the sheds to coincide with her arrival. He knew he acted like a lovesick schoolboy, but couldn't seem to stop himself. She was always polite and cool when they talked, but he knew she felt something because a pink blush blossomed in her cheeks when she saw him. Was it fear, embarrassment, or shame? Or attraction?

A male voice came from behind him. "You there. Come with me."

Matthew looked around until he spied Bernard Bretel, Marie's brother, staring at him. "Are you addressing me?"

"I said come here." Bernard yelled across the humming filleting table to Jean. "I'm taking your boy."

Jean, who had been busily salting, jerked up straight. "Taking him?"

"That's right."

Jean looked up at the brooding sky. "Now?"

"You got along without him before, you can get along without him for a couple of hours now."

Matthew wasn't sure who he should be obeying, so he watched Jean and waited for a sign from him. He knew that Jean worried about rain; if that happened, he would need every hand to get the fish under cover. The splitter and other helpers, faces studiously blank, kept working. Fillets slapped on the table, a fish head tumbled into a barrel, liver slurped into the vat. Finally Jean nodded, so Matthew, taking this as acquiescence, squatted to rinse his hands in a bucket of clean seawater.

"Hurry up, boy. I haven't got all day."

Bernard was so surly and unpleasant that, rather than being offended, Matthew was slightly amused. He admitted to himself that he wouldn't be so blasé if he didn't know his servitude was temporary. In fact, he had been expecting to be released for some days now and felt a stirring of unease at the delay.

The knot at the front of his apron had grown wet and tight. Matthew worked it loose with his fingers and pulled the leather over his head. He veered off and hung it on a peg inside the shed. When he returned, Bernard glared at him. The temptation to tease him was too great.

"So," Matthew began in a friendly tone, "Where are we going?"

"You'll speak when you're spoken to, boy."

"I'm not complaining," continued Matthew. "That's hard work they do back there. I could use a break." He grinned like an idiot.

"I'm not interested in talking to you."

Matthew looked down at his fingers. "Will my hands ever stop stinging? What if they fester? Fish aren't that clean, are they?"

"Silence."

"What am I saying? Of course they're clean; they swim in water all day. But the flies are dirty."

Bernard stomped toward the town gate, his shoulders hiked with tension. Although Matthew continued his inane blather for another five minutes, he kept a sharp eye on his surroundings. Were the soldiers alert at their stations? How many manned the ramparts? Was there a blind spot in the cannon placements? How rotten was the wood in the bridge and the mortar in the walls?

Even when they reached the quay proper, Matthew kept a pace or two behind Bernard so the man didn't see his intense interest. A steady stream of men and carts loaded with sacks of flour trudged from a wharf across the dirt to a large, stone building where barn-like doors gaped open. Matthew sidled over to the storehouse and looked inside. Casks and barrels, bags and boxes, all piled two stories high, everything from cannonballs to hardtack, easily a couple of years' worth of supplies. A saboteur could toss a burning ember into the black powder and ruin Louisbourg's chances of defense.

Bernard turned up Rue Toulouse and Matthew hopped to catch up. The town roads were in good repair, with cobbled drains on either side against the buildings and a rutted but passable road between. People milled about, some looking intent on their business, others chatting in doorways and at corners. A boy pulling an ox shouted to a maid as she draped a feather mattress out a window to air. Only a few people noticed Matthew as a stranger. They likely thought he had arrived on a fishing boat or a merchant vessel because he spoke like a Frenchman and dressed like a seaman.

A couple of blocks up from where Bernard and Matthew walked, Marie stood outside the small house rented by the Sisters of the Congregation and waited for her daughter. She listened through the open window to the drone of the girls reciting Latin verbs and imagined she could pick out Fleurie's voice, its sweet ring higher than the other students'. A brisk breeze coaxed against the wall. The air smelled of imminent rain.

Before the siege, the sisters had owned a building large enough to house a dozen boarders and all the day students the town provided, but the British had used it as a guardhouse during their occupation and had destroyed most of it. Now they were able to fit only a handful of girls in these crowded quarters. They were good women, but in dire financial need, so Marie had offered them what amounted to a bribe to accept her daughter.

Marie wondered, not for the first time, how the Sisters managed to herd all those children and keep them in line. She found her own daughter such a trial sometimes. She blamed her mother for spoiling her. If Fleurie wanted something from her grandmother, she only had to throw a tantrum and it appeared. Teanne believed that Fleurie's good looks and family connections, not an education or a sweet disposition, would win her a rich husband.

Did the loss of the *Donna Rae* mean that Fleurie would have to leave the school? In a week, maybe two, Marie's savings would be used up, and it could be months before the income started dribbling in again.

She sank on a bench next to the wall and pressed the flat of her hand against the acid gnawing in her belly. Her storehouse contained a couple of seasons' worth of some goods. Maybe if she held an auction and sold them below cost? But people would wonder why she was suddenly short of money. They'd guess about her part in the smuggling scandal.

When Bernard appeared a few yards away, Marie shrank back on the bench and tried to be invisible. She'd learned to ignore the fact that Bernard did what he wanted when he should have been working at the station. But when Matthew scuffed into view, she found herself on her feet.

"Bernard." He stopped and waited for her to approach. "What is Matthew doing here?"

Her brother smirked. "Is that his name?"

Matthew stood nearby, his arms folded across his chest, and studied her with a pensive look. He was a good foot taller than her brother, and much broader in the shoulders. Marie motioned for Bernard to step away, out of Matthew's hearing, then hissed, "He should be down at the station. It's threatening rain." Everything at a fishing station stopped abruptly to get the fish under shelter when it rained.

"I'll send him back when I'm done."

"Done what?"

"Something that has nothing to do with you."

His tone had her bristling. "How can it have nothing to do with me? You've taken one of my workers."

"Your worker? Your worker? Who's the master of that station, eh? Me." He jabbed a finger at his chest.

"It's a simple question, Bernard."

"I'll send him back when I'm done."

Marie glanced over at Matthew. Did he know what Bernard was doing? Should she ask him? No. That would only put the man in a difficult position. If he answered, he'd anger Bernard.

"I don't want you dragging him into your sidelines," she said instead. "Besides, look at the sky, Bernard."

"Why are you concerned about him, eh? You'd think he was your brother. He's British. He's nothing."

"That's not the point."

"What is the point? You're always interfering with my business, with the way I run things."

Hah, as if he ran things. "Do you blame me after what happened to the south station?" Bernard had run that business straight into the ground. It went from a thriving fishing establishment to a tumbledown building and a rotting wharf in less than a year. When the Basque fishermen arrived that spring expecting her to hire them on, she had to scramble to find them a boat with another owner.

"Bah, that wasn't my fault." He gave Matthew a come-along motion and started back up the street.

"Bernard," Marie snapped. She hated that Matthew saw this exchange. Every time she showed a weakness in front of a man, other than Quentin, Bernard capitalized on it. She had to assert herself or she lost respect, which eventually translated into financial losses. Bernard kept walking, so she said, "Matthew, return to the station."

Matthew looked from her to Bernard. "Who exactly is the boss here? You'll have to make that clear."

"I am. And when I'm not around, Jean Riverin."

"Jean!" Bernard came charging back. "That's it! That's it! I'm through being shamed by you. I'm taking my half of the business and breaking off."

He shoved her shoulder hard. Matthew was suddenly there, giving her his arm for balance. It felt rock hard under her hand before she recovered herself and snatched it away.

"Your half?" she gasped, incredulous. "You don't have a half."

"I'm owed it! Maman married you to Jubert for the family's sake, not yours alone. You have no family loyalty." Bernard turned his head and spat into the dirt.

A rock settled in Marie's chest. She narrowed the distance between them and looked her brother hard in the eye. "That's right," she said with iron in her voice. "Fifteen years old, I was. Did you speak up for me? Did you consider my feelings? No." She shook her head, disdain dripping from her words. "You led me to that marriage like a lamb to a slaughter."

"We did you a favor. You should be grateful."

"Get out of my sight." Her throat trembled with anger.

"I mean it, Marie. You sign over half the business or you'll be sorry."

He jabbed a fist toward her face, making her flinch and close her eyes. Marie felt certain he would have made contact but Matthew intervened by grabbing Bernard's wrist in mid-air.

"What do you think you're doing!" Bernard screeched at him. "Who do you think you are? You touched me! You can't touch me. You're going to pay for that."

Matthew didn't step back. In fact, Marie had the feeling that if she'd given one indication that it was her wish, he would have punched Bernard in the nose.

A bubble of voices sounded and the schoolhouse door banged open behind her. Marie didn't look around just yet. She wanted to study her brother's face. Why did he imagine she would sign over half her business to him? He knew something. Even though he now directed his anger at Matthew, she could tell he held something back. He believed that he was party to some secret, some way to make her sorry. Why? What did he know?

"Maman," a little voice squeaked imperiously. "I'm ready."

"Yes, Fleurie, I'm ready also."

As if instinctively, Matthew squatted down to be at eye level with the child. She was beautiful, Marie knew, like a dressed-up doll in her linen chemise, crisp white apron, and full overskirt. Under her ruffled white cap, black curls twirled around a shiny pink ribbon that matched the color of the stripe in her skirt. Fleurie was well aware that she was pretty. She glanced at Matthew and pointedly dismissed him as unworthy of her attention. At the same time, she preened, on display. A little kitten with sharp claws.

"I'm hungry," she said with a pretty pout.

"There's food at home, yes? We'll go get some." Marie stood behind Fleurie and put her hands on the child's shoulders to guide her away, but although Fleurie rocked at the nudge, she didn't take a step.

"I want to go to *Grand-mère*'s house. She makes me little cakes."

"She is very good to you, isn't she?" Marie nudged her shoulders again, frustration building.

Fleurie stayed put. "No, I'm not going to our house, I'm going to *Grand-mère*'s house."

"Not today. Come along."

Fleurie's eyebrows squeezed low, her mouth forming a hard pout. "No! No! No!"

Bernard chuckled, as if this little tantrum was the cutest thing he'd ever seen. "I'll take her. Come with me, Fleurie."

"No," Marie snapped. "She can't get her way every time she has a whim."

"Why not? You do."

Fleurie appeared not to notice the bitter words. "I'm going with Uncle Bernard."

"No, you're not." Marie put her hands under Fleurie's arms and hoisted her up. She wailed and squirmed, her clogs banging painfully against Marie's legs. Marie held tight and determinedly started off.

Suddenly Fleurie stilled. Marie followed her gaze. Ahead of them, Matthew walked back and forth on his hands, his short trousers sliding down to expose bulging calves that made Marie's heart jump. She averted her eyes. This was the first time Fleurie had ever seen such a trick and she was captivated. Still on his hands, Matthew moved jerkily toward the corner. Once there, he tried to manage the turn on a steep downward slope but lost his balance and fell on his rear.

Fleurie giggled. "Do it again!"

"I can't on a hill, little one. But I can carry you on my shoulder . . . if it's all right with your Maman?"

Marie smiled at him gratefully. She knew this demonstration was tantamount to rewarding Fleurie's tantrum, but at least it got them clear of Bernard. Her brother stomped up the hill, tension in every movement.

Matthew plucked Fleurie from her and effortlessly settled her on his left shoulder, his long fingers wrapped protectively around her ankles. The skin of his hand looked tanned and healthy against her daughter's long black stockings.

For the next five minutes, Fleurie kept up a stream of bright chatter, encouraged by Matthew. Marie felt strangely embarrassed and couldn't come up with anything to say.

"I'm bigger than you are, Maman."

Marie made a show of craning her neck. "Yes, you are. What can you see from way up there?"

Fences surrounded each of the house lots to protect the gardens and livestock from thieves and roaming animals. The boards next to them rose too high for Marie to see over. Fleurie, however, peered over the top.

"I see Doo-doo."

"Doo-doo?" Marie asked.

Fleurie giggled and delightful dimples appeared on each soft cheek. Her ribbons bounced and her eyes sparkled. "Monsieur Dumond's cow."

Marie's heart swelled. She dearly loved this child, even when she put on a spoiled show. At times like this, when she forgot herself, Fleurie seemed the most precious little girl ever made.

"And I see our roof."

"Your roof?" Matthew asked his little cargo.

"I live through there." She pointed to the alley running between a tall, almost windowless building and a piquet fence.

"Our garden is behind there," Marie said.

"Maman! Maman! There's Treenie!" Fleurie bounced on Matthew's shoulders and pointed over a slat board fence to her friend Treenie's house. "May I stay? Please?"

They pushed through the gate and into a garden that was part packed earth and part raised vegetable beds. After a quick conference with Treenie's mother inside the house, Fleurie scurried off to play. Matthew and Marie watched hér a moment.

"She's a beautiful child," Matthew said.

"Yes, she is. But she has a temper, that one." Embarrassed by the scene back at the school, she couldn't look him in the eye.

"She probably just sensed the tension between you and your brother and reacted to it."

Tension. That seemed a mild word for what went on between Marie and Bernard. Marie swung back through the gate to the road. Both her children were sensitive to emotions. She had no idea where they inherited that tendency.

Matthew stopped and turned around in the street as if to get his bearings. "Are we near the quay?"

"Very."

"I can't see the church tower from here."

"It's that way," Marie said, pointing.

She realized that although Matthew had been in Louisbourg for weeks, he worked at the fishing station from morning until dark and wouldn't have had time to explore the city. The next day was Sunday; perhaps he'd get a chance after Mass.

Would Matthew attend church? What a startling thought. Everyone Marie knew went to Mass. This man looked and sounded like a countryman and, despite his rough clothes, he carried himself like a nobleman. But he wasn't. He was the enemy. She'd been walking and chatting with him as if he were an old friend—or a suitor.

Suddenly Marie felt exposed and self-conscious. Two women with baskets over their arms called a pleasant greeting that she returned. She cringed inwardly. No doubt the women were now talking behind their hands, wondering who the handsome stranger was. They'd be appalled when they learned she strolled about the town with an English prisoner. And they would learn.

She crossed her arms at her chest and watched her feet. "What did Bernard need you for?"

Matthew shrugged. "He never said."

"He probably just wanted to show you off—" She stopped, aghast by her rudeness, but he only smiled. "Or he needed someone to do some physical work, like carry a barrel of rum. That one, he's not one to do something when he can get someone else to do it for him."

"It's hard to believe you're related."

She recognized the compliment. "I think he takes after our mother, and I like to believe I have my father's temperament."

"Your father lives in Louisbourg?"

"No, he died when I was ten. Lost fishing." She averted her face, embarrassed by the weight of sorrow she felt even after all these years.

"That must have been hard. How did your mother support herself?"

"My grandparents were alive then."

"And your husband?"

"Killed in the siege." She suspected that Matthew already knew that.

"I'm sorry. You must miss him."

It sometimes worried Marie that she didn't mourn her husband. In fact, his death freed her. Did that make her a bad person? Her husband had been demanding, selfish, and vain, but not cruel. "He was . . . we were not . . . ." She cleared her throat. "He was much older than me."

"So I gathered from what you said before, with your brother."

"I'm sorry you saw that, my argument with Bernard. He isn't easy, that one."

"It's none of my business, but it seems to me that you are loyal to your family. You employ him when he's obviously not—"

"Worth a single livre? As you say, he is my brother."

"He threatened you. He seemed quite confident of himself."

"Yes, he did."

"Me, I'd be worried about that."

That sounded like a friendly warning. Was this her opportunity to find out what he knew about the *Donna Rae*? She tensed and turned her head. Their eyes met and they stopped walking, simply staring at one another while the rest of the street moved and talked and shut doors. She read a question in his gaze, but also sympathy and something else, something sweeter and aching.

A wash of longing crept over her. If only he would hug her, gather her in his arms and let her breathe. She heard a small choking sound and realized with a start that it came from her own throat.

"I . . . I am concerned," she said finally.

"I would like to help you, if I can."

Chapter Six

The fragility in Marie's eyes abruptly snapped away and she demanded, "Why? Why would you want to help me?"

Matthew struggled with a response. *Because I feel responsible? Because it's the right thing to do? Because I like you?* He did like her; he liked her a lot.

"And why do you think you can?" Marie demanded when he didn't answer.

"You mean because I'm a merely a prisoner?"

"You don't know anything about me, or about my life, or my business . . . do you?"

He nodded slowly. "I crewed on the *Donna Rae*." If she was the Louisbourg contact, this was her opportunity to confide in him.

She considered him somberly. "What do you know?"

"I don't know anything. I suspect something."

"Suspect what?"

"That you have something to do with the *Donna Rae*."

"And if I did, what would you do?" Her voice sounded hard, but her eyes smoldered with anxiety and fear.

"I'd try to see that you didn't . . ." His voice trailed off.

What could he do? He'd been naïve and impetuous to offer. Perhaps, in the future, when this venture was completed, he'd have some power to help her, to shield her from the consequences of her actions. But now?

"Would you tell anyone I was involved? Report me to the authorities?" she asked.

"No, of course not," he gasped. The very thought made him bristle indignantly.

He suddenly considered that response. Why wouldn't he expose her? A few months earlier he had believed smuggling was amoral, that it unraveled the economic fabric of the countries involved. That had been one of the considerations in his impulsive decision to make this trip. What had changed?

He now knew the people involved, of course. His sympathy for them grew partly because the authorities here generally turned a blind eye to smuggling, so it had become commonplace. Rather than ostracizing smugglers, Louisbourgeois relied on them for basic goods like building supplies. They faced hardships and scarcity here unknown in Europe. Especially now, when the citizens struggled to rebuild what had been destroyed in the war.

"Then perhaps you could be of service to me." Marie glanced up and down the street and started walking. "I'd like to talk to Captain Martin. Do you see him?"

He smiled grimly, recalling the cramped benches that he and the other prisoners slept on every night. "I can talk to him." He frowned. "He doesn't much like me, that one."

"But he's working on the west rampart? I've seen him head that way."

"At the base of them, I think. On the outer wall."

"So he must know where the lime kiln is."

Matthew had seen it on his daily walks to and from the King's Bastion. "Yes."

"Tell Gabe I'll be there after Mass tomorrow, Sunday."

The familiar way she said his name made Matthew twitch his shoulder, uncomfortable. Did she have a relationship with him? He remembered the way Captain Martin had stared at her the day they arrived, when the tender pulled in to the wharf.

"Do you know Captain Martin well? Are you friends?" he asked, a little too forcefully.

She appeared to consider this. "No, not a friend. He's English, a Protestant."

"But you do business with him, this Englishman?"

She shot him a sidelong look. "And the schooner you worked on did business with a Frenchman. It's profits, not politics."

"Even after what happened to you in the war?"

She narrowed her eyes. "And what do you know about what I went through?"

"You said yourself you lost your husband then."

She increased her pace, obviously uncomfortable with the turn of conversation. The street on which they had been traveling ended at the wide quay and the harbor. Three soldiers made a triangle at the corner, one in the sentry box, the other two leaning on the barrels of their muskets.

"Those soldiers are looking at you like they know who you are," Marie hissed, widening the gap between them by taking a long stride forward.

Although the prisoners were permitted to roam the town, at the request of their respective employers, they were still watched carefully. The men in the garrison took pains to know each of them by sight.

"I'll leave you here then, Madame?" he asked politely.

"Yes, go back to the station immediately." She looked up at the gunmetal gray belly of the sky. Jean Riverin would need every available hand to get the fish under cover before the rain.

Chin raised, she didn't even bother looking at Matthew, just glided away as if she had already dismissed him from her mind. In truth, Marie had to fight the urge to turn and watch him walk away. She thought of little else these days. It shamed her that she seemed incapable of blocking him from her mind, she who knew better than to allow the vulnerability.

Marie considered herself a very disciplined woman. She had had to be to survive the last six years with her family intact. This preoccupation with the man had to end. Now.

The only reason she had arranged for him to work for her was to watch him to see if he intended to turn her in and to use him as a go-between with Gabe Martin. That was accomplished. She didn't need Matthew anymore. The next time he hailed her at the fishing station, she would nod abruptly and turn away. No more peeking at him through the cottage door, watching him at work. No more admiring the way his face changed when he smiled. No more anticipating each morning because he would be there.

Sadness dropped over her mood like a stifling blanket. She felt bereft, which was nonsense, of course. Matthew was a means to an end, nothing more.

Marie had walked three houses past the butcher's before she realized where she was. She marched back and ordered the next week's meat for her home and for the fishing station.

When she emerged, the sky had darkened further and whitecaps dotted the harbor waters. She thought about going back up the hill and fetching Fleurie before the rain started, but then realized that it would be shorter to cut through her own garden. The wind stole her breath and wrapped her skirts around her legs.

Suddenly a deep boom rocked the ground. Instantly terrified, Marie bolted toward home. Her mind blazed with only one thought: her babies. Save her babies! The bombs . . . Then reality surfaced.

"Oh . . . oh . . . thunder," she mumbled. "Just thunder."

She slowed and caught her breath. Her heart felt like a drum roll in her chest. Had anyone else seen her sudden gallop? Her gaze roamed up and down the quay. Two children rolled metal barrel hoops along the road, but they were oblivious to everything but their game. A couple of sailors sat on the grassy bank, watching her. No matter; they were strangers.

This wasn't the first time she had panicked at thunder—it sounded so like the bombardment of 1745, when her mother country was at war with England and the American colonists had attacked Louisbourg. She reacted instinctively. The siege came rushing back as if she'd been thrust into it all again. The thumps, then long seconds while she held her breath and hunched protectively over Claude, her baby. When the crash of impact came, she felt only relief, not worry about where the bomb had landed. Just relief that the baby inside her and the child in her arms had survived.

She had given birth to Fleurie during a bombardment, a horrible experience that she often relived in nightmares. She would make with a scream, soaked in perspiration.

That day the air had vibrated with thunderous whines, roars, and crashes. Every few minutes her bed rocked and grit fell from the ceiling onto her face, blinding her until tears blinked her eyes clear. The midwife had intended to move her to a cellar, but the contractions came on suddenly and hard, one on top of the other. Her body screamed in agony, as if it would tear into pieces. Then a bomb hit on the street outside. Its reverberations threw the midwife against a wall and blew Marie's bed onto its side. As she fought the suffocating blankets and mattress, another contraction gripped her.

Fleurie came into the world surrounded by screams and dirt and smoke and terror.

The British had done that, specifically the men from New England. During the siege she had cursed them day after day. How could she possibly have feelings for one of them now? Because he sounded and acted and looked like a Frenchman? Probably.

The rain started, first as dark spots on the cobbles, then in fat drops that smacked her face, driven sideways by the wind. A humid, almost sweet smell rose from the earth. Marie darted through the front door of her cottage.

"Caught in the rain, eh? Me, I'm glad to work inside," Quentin said, looking up from where he'd been counting out hooks.

Marie stood looking out the door, shivering in the damp chill. She could barely see the house across the street for the slanting rain. "It sounds like . . . the siege."

"I've thought so many times."

Quentin sounded melancholy so Marie turned and

considered him. He hunched over the desk, his thick shoulders rounded. She had to remember that her worries were, for the most part, his as well. He depended on her for his employment. Also, he considered her a friend, almost a daughter.

"Why don't you go home to your family, yes?" she said. "I'll be here the rest of the day. No use checking on the station in this weather."

Down at the fishing station, Matthew grabbed one end of the top of a slat table. A quick count to three to coordinate their movements and not tip the fish onto the ground, and he and the other *garçon* hoisted the top from its legs like a giant tray from a table. The two of them struggled over the rocky shoreline toward the cottage.

The tables had been built narrow enough to pass through the low door, but with little room to spare, so Matthew tore skin from his knuckle on the rough door frame. When the fish were safely stacked, he paused to lick the sting out of his hand. It tasted of salt.

"That all of them?" Jean asked.

Matthew nodded. "Not much room in here now, eh?"

"No. We could use another shed or some more canvas." Jean leaned his forearm on the door frame and peered out into the rain. "Hope this doesn't last. A couple of summers ago, it rained all the time. Lost a lot of fish that year."

Matthew couldn't see a bench, or even a square of dirt, to sit on. "What would you like me to do now?"

Jean watched the other *garçon* scurry out the back door toward the bunkhouse. "You can go, but if it lets up, you come back here, eh?"

"There won't be any trouble about that? About me being unsupervised during the day?" He hoped he wouldn't be required to return to the prison.

"No. Me, I'd go to the tavern, if I were you. Do you have any money?"

"No livre."

Jean disappeared into his private room and emerged a moment later jingling some coins. "You take these. You've earned them."

Matthew thanked him and shoved the coins into his pocket. He had no idea of what things cost here, but he longed for a quiet meal accompanied by a glass of good wine.

"Before you go, Matthew," Jean said, "what did Bernard need you for?"

"I never found out. Madame Jubert saw me with him and sent him off. She told me to come back here." That sounded mild compared to the actual incident, the ferocious argument between Marie and her brother.

Jean smiled. "She's brave, that one."

"You admire her."

One shoulder bounced in a shrug but Jean averted his eyes furtively. "In business, yes? She's good in business."

"And ambitious?" Matthew probed.

"She has to be. You heard what happened to her husband?"

"He died in the siege."

Matthew wanted to encourage Jean to talk, so he leaned against the wall and crossed his legs at the ankle. Jean immediately settled his rear on the edge of the table.

"After the deportation, she went to his family in France, you know, her mother- and father-in-law? They turned her away. She had her two babies and her mother and her good-for-nothing—"

He caught himself. "Her brother. That rich man's family just sent them off like they were beggars." He shook his head sadly. "Their own grandbabies."

"Did they have no one else? What about her mother's family?"

"Bah, all from here or somewhere else in Isle Royale. She's third-generation Canadian."

"Where did she go? How did they survive?"

Jean wrapped his arms tightly across his chest. "I heard from someone who saw Bernard Bretel in Paris that they lived in poverty. All of them—mother, brother, babies—in a single room in a garret."

It was all too easy to imagine the squalor. Matthew's heart ached for her. "For how long?"

"Three years."

Matthew sighed heavily. "Three years."

"And when they did get back here, there was almost nothing left. Roofs off houses. Rubble in the streets. Almost no fishing boats."

"The English took them?"

Jean cocked his eyebrow. "The English? You say that as if you're not one with them."

Matthew pushed off the wall. "I am French."

"Me, I don't care either way," Jean replied with a shrug. But his look belied his words as he stared at Matthew long and hard.

Chapter Seven

Shoulders hunched against the rain, Matthew jogged down the quay toward the building where he'd seen the spruce bough draped over the sign. The bough meant that the establishment served spruce beer and other alcoholic beverages.

He scuffed up the few steps, opened the door, and walked into a blast of heat and pipe smoke. The cramped room was fifteen paces by ten paces and filled with long plank tables and benches. A broad-ended woman leaned over the roaring fire, scooping from a black cauldron.

Matthew closed the door behind him and shook the rain from his shoulders. Then he inhaled, letting the familiar smells and warmth wash over him. Port taverns, it seemed, were the same the world over. Here the words were primarily spoken in French, but the accents came from everywhere.

There were fishermen with tanned faces and toques over greasy hair, off-duty soldiers gambling away their earnings, and the crew of a merchant ship who seemed to be speaking in a guttural-sounding German. No one here, Matthew realized, would think him anything other than a French sailor. It felt liberating.

Apparently he wasn't the only one taking shelter from the rain; the benches were crowded with men talking, smoking, eating, and playing cards. He caught the eye of a nearby sailor and the man shifted down the bench, making room. They exchanged a greeting before the man bent back over his food.

When the waitress shuffled over with a weary smile on her chubby cheeks, Matthew ordered a jug of sweet cider, heated, and a platter of bread and cheese. He had heard that the prices in the town were higher than in Europe, so he ordered modestly to be sure he had enough money. When the cider arrived, he closed his eyes and let the sharp cinnamon flavor fill his senses. A half-moon of dark bread sat before him and Matthew almost chuckled. It was exactly the same fare they ate every morning in the prison cell, heavy and dry but nutty and filling.

Soon the food, cider, and warmth worked together to loosen the tense muscles in his shoulders and neck. He imagined his friends back home, and what they would think if they saw him now. They might think him a fool, or they might admire his courage and be proud of his sacrifice. He wasn't proud of himself. Oh, his intentions had been good in the beginning, but he accepted the challenge offered to him all those months ago without giving it the consideration it warranted, without thinking of the lives of the people he would affect. He'd only thought of himself and the longing within him for adventure.

Matthew had always felt he had an average temperament: open to new ideas, but not an easy mark; brave but not foolhardy; intelligent but not brilliant; considerate but not remarkably so. This experience taught him differently. He was an easy mark to men who approached him with an idea for adventure. He had felt fear more than a few times these last months. For all his book learning, he never understood the reality of smuggling. And he'd been anything but considerate to the people affected by the seizure of the *Donna Rae*.

Marie Jubert had carried more than enough hardship in her life before he came along. During the argument with her brother, she said she'd been married off to an elderly man at the age of fifteen. Just a girl. Considering that she had a seven-year-old son, Matthew decided that Marie was probably only twenty-four years old now. Five years younger than he was, and so much more experienced in the ways of the world. He'd never met a woman with such a drive for success. In spite of all that, a layer of fragility and sadness lived in the depths of her eyes. Was she lonely? Probably.

Could it be true that Capitaine Jerome de Monluc meant to marry Marie? She'd be a fool to tether herself to such a shallow, cruel man. He'd take over her business, her wealth. She would belong to him. Matthew gritted his teeth. She deserved a kind man, one who would love her with every breath he took and cherish her children as if they were his own blood.

He could be such a man. He squeezed his eyes shut in a sudden pain. Impossible. What an absurd thought. Far too many barriers blocked the way. Suddenly the air smelled stale and the bench felt hard. He downed the last of his drink and headed back out into the storm. It was only as he tromped through the muck that he began to wonder where he should go.

He decided to find the other prisoners. Most of them spent their days repairing the fortress walls. No doubt there were things they could do in the rain, such as fetch boulders and dig trenches, but the actual laying of the rock involved mortar. As far as he knew, the others hadn't yet been given spending money so he doubted that they found shelter in a tavern.

Thunder rumbled and rain fell in sheets off the slate roofs. Water and foul things rushed down the hills along cobbled gutters running between the streets and the buildings, gurgling along trenches cut into the quay to eventually empty into the harbor.

Matthew paused at the head of the Frederic Gate and stared across the water. Waves sloshed against the wharf, trailing white arcs of foam. Beyond that, dozens of ships hunkered gray and ghostly in the driving rain. He trudged up the Rue Toulouse with mud sucking at his feet.

It took only a quarter of an hour for Matthew to find Gabe Martin. He and Tom Smith hunkered down next to a small fire in the lee of a gun emplacement. Nearby, a mound of boulders waited by a half-repaired wall.

Matthew squatted beside them and held his palms toward the fire. His fingers throbbed blue with cold.

"Gave you the afternoon off too, eh?" Tom asked in English.

"Can't dry fish in the rain." Matthew settled on a block of stone. "The shoremaster gave me a handful of coins so I went to a tavern."

"Well, that was right generous of him. I could do with a swill of grog, and that's the truth."

Matthew scooped the few coins left in his pocket and showed them to Tom. "Is that enough for a grog?"

"Lord love us—"

"Tom!"

"Quiet!"

Both Matthew and Captain Martin snapped at once. Then they looked about to be sure none of the locals had heard him. It was a wonder that Tom hadn't already been caught taking the Lord's name in vain.

"Awk! I'm sorry."

"Remember," Captain Martin said sternly, "if one of us is charged, we all face the punishment."

"We've got to teach you some non-blasphemous swear words," Matthew added.

Tom nodded. "Something the locals are used to hearing."

"We French swear differently than you English," Matthew explained. "The worst thing you can call a man is a thief, and the worst thing you can say to a woman is that she has loose morals. Understand? So that's how we swear."

"I've been called a . . ." Tom paused to twist his tongue around the foreign sounding word. "*Voleur.* That means thief, right?"

"Yes. They're probably not really saying you're a thief; it's just a way of cursing."

The three of them traded French swear words for a few minutes. At one point, a soldier happened to be passing. He looked shocked at the charge that he, or someone else nearby, was a *cranky girl*. That gave Tom, Matthew, and Captain Martin a chuckle, the first one in over a week. The captain seemed to be the first to recall their situation. His face sober, he leaned down to pull at his boot leather.

"Listen, Tom," Matthew said after they settled down. "I want to have a word with the captain. How about you take the rest of this money and go buy yourself a pint?"

Tom's eyebrows bounced up. "I've been hankering for one." He looked to Captain Martin.

"Go ahead. But no swearing, mind. And no getting so drunk you miss curfew."

Tom grabbed the coins and took off at a bent jog.

"What was so important that you were willing to give up ready money?" Captain Martin asked, reaching for another handful of twigs.

"Madame Jubert."

His hand paused in mid-air for a second before dropping the twigs on the fire. "What about her?"

"She asked me to pass on a message to you."

Captain Martin peered at him suspiciously. "She did."

"She said she'd meet you at the lime kiln tomorrow, after Mass."

"Why would she send you to tell me that?"

"I work for her."

"It's a peculiar request."

It hadn't occurred to Matthew that the captain wouldn't believe him. Did he think it a trap? "I'd go if I were you. What would be the harm? No one said we weren't allowed to move about the town on Sundays. It's a day of rest, after all. And if you happen to run into the widow . . . ?"

"You've become friendly with her?"

Matthew heaved an expressive shrug. "I see her every day. We exchange greetings."

"And that's all?"

"What more could there be?" He hoped his face didn't give away how he really felt.

"Yet she confided in you?" he growled.

Matthew threw a twig like a spear into the fire. "She asked me to pass on a message."

"But you have your suspicions?"

"Of course I do. Was it a coincidence that her shore-master hired me? I don't think so. She wanted a prisoner who could speak French so she could find out what's going on."

Captain Martin snorted. "Why did you sign on with the *Donna Rae* in the first place? There were other vessels in the port that day. What made you choose us?"

"I needed the work."

"You're obviously an educated man. Strong enough, but when you started you had no calluses on your hands. I didn't think that was important before we were arrested. Now I'm wondering."

"What are you suggesting? That I like being a prisoner? That I arranged all this so I could salt fish all day?"

"There is that," Captain Martin conceded. "If you set us up, you'd be a free man now. Unless you're stupid?"

I am stupid, Matthew thought. He stared into the fire and asked, "What is the date?"

Captain Martin looked taken aback. "Today's date? I'm not sure. The first week in May. Why?"

"It's cold here in May," Matthew mumbled vaguely.

"Yes, well, I'm missing my home port too."

In truth, Matthew was thinking about the ship that should have arrived in Louisbourg before now, the ship that Captain Martin knew nothing about. It promised to solve one of Matthew's problems but create another in its wake. Had it been lost at sea? Or diverted to a distant port? Surely if the authorities knew that there would be a delay they would have sent word somehow.

Captain Martin heaved himself to his feet. "I'd best catch up with Tom. Keep an eye on him."

"Good idea." Matthew liked Tom Smith very much but he had to agree that the man tended to be erratic and loud outside the confines of the ship's bells. A bit of mischievousness could be taken as good fun in most ports, but here . . . ? Matthew ran his tongue along his bottom teeth. Here the consequences could be very grim indeed.

He pulled his collar around his ears and hugged his knees to his chest. From this spot he looked out over the moor: rocks, scraggy shrubs in brilliant new green, twisted fir trees, and mist rising in eerie clouds silhouetting the hillocks. Desolate, yes, but also throat-catchingly beautiful.

Early Sunday morning, Matthew looked up through the corroded bars on the cell window toward white puffs of clouds drifting across a pale blue sky. Behind him the other men stared hopefully out to the passageway, waiting for the guard to release them for the day. The previous night's storm had been hard. Water seeped through the walls and soaked the plank benches that they slept on. Tempers flared. Only Captain Martin's steady leadership kept the men from throwing fists.

"He's coming," someone said.

As soon as the door creaked open, the other men

crowded out, but Matthew stayed put. Sunday. The day of rest. He had nowhere to go and plenty of reason to remain.

Suddenly the church bells high above him gonged, calling the faithful to Mass. As the sound reverberated though his body, Matthew closed his eyes and composed himself. He couldn't attend, but he would be able to hear the service and likely smell the incense.

He climbed to the second level of the benches and leaned his back on the damp inner wall, out of sight of the people passing by the door, and looked down at the dirt embedded in the folds of his knuckles and around his nails. He longed for a sliver of soap and a bucket of hot water. It seemed sacrilegious to be attending church in this state, though he supposed God would forgive him, considering the situation.

Soon the parishioners began to arrive at the Chapelle de Saint-Louis, talking, laughing, feet crunching on the gravel outside and then scuffing along the stones of the echoing passageway. No doubt Marie and her children moved among them. He'd never seen her son. Did he look like Marie? Her daughter did. Matthew smiled; what a feisty little doll. Fleurie was going to break men's hearts when she grew up.

Eventually the movement outside his door stilled and the people inside the church were silent except for the occasional creak of wood and muffled cough. When the Mass began, Matthew clasped his hands together and strained to hear the priest's voice. The Latin washed over him. The incense filled his nostrils. He felt comforted by the ritual.

"Here you are." Tom Smith's voice broke in. "What are you doing?"

Matthew dropped his clasped hands guiltily. "Tom."

"Were you praying along with them across the way? Them Catholics?"

"I was praying." Matthew admitted no more than that as he scooted off the bench. "You were looking for me?"

Tom still looked confused, but he held up a ball of twine with a hook tied to one end. "One of the soldiers lent me this. Thought we might catch something for dinner."

"Sounds good to me." Matthew, eager to distract Tom, headed for the door. "There must be a stream or river nearby." He thought about a fresh trout frying in a bubble of fat and his stomach growled. It was a perfect time of year to catch them, although a bit late in the morning.

"Any inside the walls will be fished out. Think they'll let us outside?"

"Probably not." Matthew hurried down the passageway toward the sunlight. "Me, I'm pretty tired of cod, but if we must, we can jig a line off the wharf."

"Where will we cook it?"

"I'm not sure," Matthew replied. "A fire on the beach? Or we might be able to trade fish for dinner."

"Or rum!" Tom snorted a laugh.

* * *

When the Mass ended, Marie, rather than lingering about to talk to her neighbors as was her custom, clasped her children's hands and left the church. As she passed it, she saw that the door to the cell stood open. Although she didn't look inside, she knew—as did all the people of Louisbourg—that was where Matthew and the other prisoners spent their nights. The air smelled of dampness and body odor.

She felt a slight nausea, nervous about her meeting with Captain Martin. Would he be there? Did Matthew pass on her message? That morning she'd chosen a heavy lace shawl to go over her head to obscure much of her face. She left it on despite the warm spring day.

From the King's Bastion she headed past the guardhouse then left down the Rue Petit Etang, skirting the puddles from the previous night's rain.

"Why are we going this way?" Claude asked.

"It's a lovely day," Marie answered, glad to have a ready excuse. "We'll go the long way. Enjoy the sun, yes?"

These days Claude felt too grown up to hold his mother's hand, so he soon shook free and scurried ahead. He ran with the exuberance of a child, fast as he could go, arms bent so his hands punched the air with each stride. They were very good in church, her little ones. They did squirm, yes, and swing their feet forward and backward, but what child didn't?

"He's going to get his Sunday clothes dirty," Fleurie

said, watching her brother gallop up a steep grassy
bank, his feet slipping on the dewy green.

"Perhaps it's all right this once. Do you want to play
with him?"

"Uh-huh!" Fleurie tore off.

Marie smiled. There had been little chance for her
children to frolic on the grass this spring; the snows had
left the ground only a scant few weeks earlier. Besides,
this gave her an excuse to linger around the lime kiln.
Not that she needed to wait; Captain Martin had already arrived. She didn't look at him directly but
moved around to the far side, between the kiln and the
steep bank that rose toward the wall. Then she bent to
pick a bouquet of fuzzy yellow flowers rising above
stiff stalks.

"Madame Jubert, you're looking well."

Not for the first time, she felt thankful that Captain
Martin spoke fluent French. "Oh Gabe, I'm so sorry
this has happened to you."

"And to you as well."

He looked tired and grubby, but not ill used. "How
are you faring?"

"Oh well," he mumbled, scuffing the toe of one boot
into the dirt. "It's not as bad as it might be. We've pretty
much got the run of the town as long as we do our work
and go back to the cell at night."

"I saw you working on the wall the other day."

Gabe just looked down at the palms of his hands. "At
least it's outdoors."

Marie took a second to assure herself that she there weren't any other adults about. The children still galloped up and down the bank, racing from the ramparts to the street and back again. Two little boys, still in their childhood skirts, were tumbling a little further along.

"Gabe, I need to know if there's anything on board the *Donna Rae* that could implicate me."

"I've thought long on that, and I'm afraid there might be."

Marie blanched. "We took such care."

"True, but I couldn't help thinking, when he was questioning me, that Capitaine de Monluc knows something. He said *she* at one point. '*How do you contact her?*' Other times he said *he* or *him*, so I'm not sure he wasn't trying to trip me up."

"Did he assume it was someone in Louisbourg?"

"Yeah. He'd been tipped off somehow."

"Warned? Where? By whom? Someone here or someone on your end?"

"I don't know. This trip started as any other."

"Did you see anyone suspicious at Canso?"

"No, I didn't make it as far as the town. They took us in Tor Bay just after we offloaded from the big ship. We never touched ground until we got hauled off here."

So they did have the contraband on board. She knew that, and yet somewhere deep inside her heart she had harbored a hope that it wasn't the case.

"You never even went ashore?" she asked. "But someone told the soldiers that you would be in Tor Bay?"

He shrugged. "We're not the only ones who use the shelter there. Some even go brazenly into Canso to do the transfer."

"What about that other ship, the one you offloaded from? Did Capitaine de Monluc accost her?"

"He just let her go. She'd sailed out of sight, then the brig appeared and blocked the harbor entrance."

Marie remembered that she was supposed to be picking flowers and bent to the task. "Was there anything on board that carried my mark? My double loop?"

"I don't think so, but I can't be sure. It's possible that someone—a crew member from the last trip, say—stole something, kept a souvenir." He hastened to add, "It's not likely, just possible."

"Were any of the casks or bails opened this time, or on any earlier trips? I'm thinking that my mark might have been on a bit of canvas or something?" She knew the cargo was supposed to be off-limits to the crew, but mischief happened.

He sighed and shook his head. "I'm sorry, Marie. I don't think so but I can't be sure. It's not like it hasn't happened before. One time I found a barrel stave with a mark from one of the American suppliers. It was jammed in a door to keep it from banging. Those things happen no matter how careful I am."

"Oh, Gabe, I'm not blaming you. How are your men coping?"

"It's hard on them, but we expect to be ransomed soon."

"I'll try to get word to the partners to hurry things along."

"Please don't take any risks. The governor's clerks have things in motion."

"You'll let me know if you think of anything I should know?"

He frowned. "I can get word through Matthew Carter."

Something in his voice had her asking, "What?"

He paused a moment before answering. "He signed on just as we were leaving Portsmouth. I don't know. Something about the man . . . ."

Marie's heart jolted and she asked, a little too loudly, "You think there's something suspicious about Matthew?"

"No . . . no . . . not really. It just seemed a bit convenient that I had a free berth at that time. One of the crew didn't turn up."

Marie reminded herself that she'd known Matthew for less than a week, not enough time to say she knew him well. Did he have anything to do with the seizure? Her heart told her no. Besides, if he were the leak, he wouldn't be locked up with the others right now. He'd be spending the reward money.

"Could that other sailor be the one who talked? The man you said didn't turn up?"

His shoulder bobbed. "He didn't seem the type, but if he was bribed? Money speaks loudly."

"We'll probably never know what happened."

He looked around. "I better leave you before someone wonders what we're doing back here."

She smiled her thanks and he disappeared around the corner.

Marie realized that she'd been compulsively tearing apart the flowers in her hands. She threw them aside. Something green and sticky stained her palms.

By now, the *Donna Rae* had been moored in Louisbourg harbor for almost a week, plenty of time for the soldiers to search it. If they found any incriminating evidence, she would have heard about it. Unless the authorities were keeping it a secret while they built a case against her.

Maybe Capitaine de Monluc had his own personal reasons for keeping it to himself. She would have to talk to Jerome again and question him covertly but carefully. The man had the morals of a bottom feeder, and a brilliant mind, but he was also profoundly arrogant. She could use his conceit as a weapon, a way to gain his confidence without him knowing. But didn't that make her just as amoral as he?

This is all my own fault. When she entered the smuggling business, she had rationalized all her moral doubts away. She did it for her children, didn't she? She needed the money so they could both get good educations and make good marriages and have the option of living wherever they chose, with whomever they chose. Her children would have the freedom she never had.

Was that the whole reason? If she were to be honest with herself, Marie had to admit that there were other attractions. She wanted money for herself too, money that would keep her independent. Lots of people smuggled, and until now the authorities had turned a blind eye, but she knew the risk.

Fleurie came bounding toward her, her hands and the hem of her dress dark with mud. Her precious little face glowed.

"Mama, who was that man?"

"What man, sweetheart?" She dropped to a squat and grabbed one of Fleurie's hands, a sure way to distract the child. "Did you scrape yourself?"

Fleurie's face blanched. "Did I?" She snatched back her hand and inspected it carefully.

Marie gathered her into a hug and squeezed her own eyes closed. What if Fleurie mentioned the man to her Uncle Bernard?

Her dear children needed protection. She would do whatever it took to keep them safe.

Chapter Eight

Matthew eyed the pond critically. It was a good size to be inside the town walls, almost a lake. No buildings abutted it, no latrines were nearby. The soil around it was thin and mounded with granite boulders so chances were good that the pond had a deep center. He left Tom scrounging for something to use as bait and walked the water's edge. This time of year the water was high and a number of lively streams emptied into the still water. A sturdy bridge crossed a narrow section, leapfrogging from rock to island until it reached the other side.

Even in the height of a dry summer, Louisbourg would always have fresh drinking water. That must have been a comfort during the siege.

When Matthew and the other prisoners were led off the *Donna Rae* they had each toted a knapsack with personal items, including an extra cotton shirt, a pair of leggings for very cold days, a hooded cloak, and a blanket. Matthew contrived to rinse one of his shirts every day, even though the water was already mucky from use. Now that he had a free day, he was determined to freshen up his body as well.

He climbed behind a large boulder and sloshed through the water to hunker down out of sight. After ensuring that no one was looking, he shrugged off his waistcoat and hauled his chemise over his head. His neckerchief stood in for a washcloth. He splashed and scrubbed until his hair dripped and his skin glowed red. Once he had dressed again, he pulled his fingers through his hair and tied it back with a leather thong. Then he captured a few minnows and carried them back to Tom Smith.

Tom knelt on a rocky ledge, leaning forward from the waist to peer into the water below. When he heard Matthew he looked up and asked, "Where ya been all this time?"

"Washing." Matthew held out his cupped hands so Tom could see the squirming minnows. "We can use these for bait, yes?"

Tom took the bait and jammed them into his pocket. "We ain't gonna catch nothing here. That lad over there was laughing at me."

Matthew scanned the pond's bank. "No other sign of fishermen. Should we try the harbor?"

"Aye."

"You want to have a wash first?" he asked.

"Naw. I ain't likely to find a lady friend around here." He pulled his line from the water and wound it around the stick.

As they scuffed down the road toward the harbor, Tom asked, "You ever think about hightailing it out of here?"

"No. And I hope you're not thinking of it either. Who knows what the punishment would be for the rest of us if someone escaped."

"It just doesn't seem right to settle in like this."

"You're not a soldier, Tom. These people aren't the enemy."

"Easy for you to say, being French and all."

"It's not so bad for us."

Tom scoffed. "Wait until winter. Got to be cold in that cell."

"Winter? We'll be home by then."

"Ha. I heard of fellas waiting years."

Matthew pictured Louisbourg in the winter and blanched. He didn't think the crew would still be prisoners by then, but if they were, he'd see to it that they had warm clothes and firewood. Somehow.

Even on a Sunday, the quay was thronged with people, mostly off-duty sailors and soldiers by the look of the mishmash of uniforms. Tom and Matthew chose one of the merchants' wharves and settled down on one end with their feet dangling over the water. Tom unrolled his string and caught the hook as it swung in the air. After baiting it, he dropped it into the water.

"How deep ya figger—" Tom stopped mid-sentence. The line had gone taut in his hand. "She's a big one!"

Hand over fist, they hauled up the fish and left it gasping on the stained boards. It was mottled, as long as Matthew's arm, and had a large mouth and flat head.

"Ugly," Matthew said as he watched the fish's tail slap languidly against the boards. "What is it?"

He immediately regretted the question, and hoped that Tom wouldn't wonder why a man who lived in New England didn't know what this fish was.

Tom barked a laugh. "You never seen a sculpin before?"

"I'm not sure. Is it good to eat?"

"Yeah, but ya got to watch these spines here. They'll give you a smart sting."

Tom peered into the fish's cavernous mouth, reached in a hand, and pulled out the hook. Matthew squatted down, grabbed the fish by the lower jaw, and dropped it quickly in a nearby half barrel.

"We must have gone too deep. I'll shorten the line some. You want a turn here?" Tom asked as he baited the hook.

"No, I'm going to move around."

"Haul us up some mussels for bait, will ya?"

A clear, warm spring day was such a rare and fleeting thing that Marie decided to take her children for a picnic out on the moor. She packed a few tightly corked bottles of sorbec, a sweetened chicken bouillon her children enjoyed, some bread, sugared nuts, and chocolate biscuits.

"I will carry the basket, Maman," Claude insisted.

The bottles made the load heavy, so Marie said, "Why don't I take one side?"

Claude shook his head. "Papa would want me to do it."

Papa? Claude was only a toddler when his father had died. Marie felt quite certain he had no memory of the man. She had always promised herself that she would never speak poorly of Yves Jubert in her children's hearing. They had no blood relatives on their father's side living in Louisbourg, and the ones in Paris refused to acknowledge them at all. So where had this sudden interest come from? Her grandmother, no doubt. Teanne Bretel had worshiped Yves. Marie often wished her mother, had married him insted.

Claude struggled out the door with both arms wrapped around the basket.

"Claude," Marie started, unsure of how to begin. "Have you been talking to someone about your papa? Because you know, if you have questions, I can answer them, yes?"

"I don't know." Claude replied with such an elaborate shrug that Marie felt quite sure the boy did have a lot of questions.

Fleurie dawdled in the kitchen, lingering by the back door. She pulled a weed out from under the lavender that grew in a gray knot beside the granite stoop. The new growth smelled so strongly it was almost bitter. She tucked a twig into the knot of her scarf at her throat.

"Fleurie!" her brother hollered.

"I'm getting my dolly." Finally she appeared dragging the doll by one hand. Although they'd all changed out of their church clothes, worse for wear after their frolic on the hillside that morning, Fleurie still insisted on ribbons in her bonnet.

Marie latched the door to keep out flies, and took Fleurie's hand as they made their way down the alley behind the house toward the back road. They meant to call upon Paulette before leaving the town walls. As she passed the warehouse Marie automatically tried the door to be sure that it was locked. The padlock hung securely bolted.

Paulette must have told the family's slave to watch for them, as she was sitting on a bench near the street. She bent from the waist and picked at a hole in her shoe. Her skin was darker than the Micmac Indians native to Isle Royale, like the pale mahogany wood in one of Marie's sideboards, so when she smiled her teeth looked unnaturally white. She saw Marie and the children approaching, grinned at them, then scurried into the imposing stone house.

Paulette emerged quickly, carrying a small basket with a white cloth tucked around the mound within. "Doughnuts," she announced. Both of the children grinned.

They made their way slowly down the street, Claude struggling with the basket in the lead. It seemed that most of Louisbourg enjoyed the sun that day. Either they sat on the benches outside their doors, or leaned out the windows talking to people on the street level. Mattresses were draped out of the upper windows, airing in the fine weather.

"Mama, Mama!" Fleurie chirped. "The hand man." She took off at a jerky skip down the hill toward the quay.

The hand man? Marie thought. Then she jerked to a stop. *Matthew*. A moment later, Fleurie hugged her doll and looked way up at the handsome man in the cut-off trousers. He dropped to a squat, his back straight, his hands dangling between his knees.

"Marie?"

At the sound of Paulette's voice, Marie realized she'd been standing there in the middle of the street.

"Who's that?"

"He's . . ." she lowered her voice and hurried to join her friend. "He's a prisoner I took on to work at the station."

"Whew, he's handsome."

"Yes, he is." His hair looked damp and clean, as did his hands and face. His rolled-up sleeves exposed muscular forearms, and his hands moved as he talked.

"He speaks French?"

She nodded. "A Protestant."

Paulette sighed, disappointed. "Such a waste."

By now they'd reached the quay proper and caught

up to the children just as Matthew smiled up at Claude. "You must be Monsieur Claude Jubert?"

"Who are you?"

"My name is Matthew Carter."

"Monsieur Carter works in my station," Marie explained. For some reason, she hesitated to tell Claude that the man was an English prisoner.

"Perhaps," Matthew said to Claude as he rose slowly, "as I am in the employ of your family, you would permit me to carry your basket for you?"

Claude glanced back, but Marie assumed an indifferent face. If she encouraged him to give up the burden, he'd probably insist on carrying it himself. Instead he lowered the basket to the street and stepped back.

Marie, Matthew, Paulette, and the children picked their way around the bogs and granite outcroppings to the west of the fortress toward the shoreline on the ocean side. It had been cleared of trees years ago, judging by the rotting stumps, and rough poles bridged the wider streams and bogs. They walked for a long time along a narrow, snaking path, away from the imposing stone walls, before nearing scraggly trees.

Claude squeaked, excited, "Look! There."

Matthew followed the boy's finger and saw a flock of ruffed grouse perched amid the nearly bare branches of a wind-twisted fir. He thought them remarkably attractive, larger than he was used to, perhaps twice the weight of a pigeon. As they approached, the male birds puffed up their chocolate-colored neck feathers and fanned their tails, but they didn't squawk and flap away as other birds would.

Claude stopped, felt around at his feet for a pebble, and pulled a slingshot from his deep jacket pocket. Matthew watched him, impressed by the boy's concentration as he readied his weapon.

Suddenly Marie said, "Claude, no!"

"Maman. They're so stupid. They'll just sit there and I can kill them all. Don't you want to eat them?"

"I do, my sweet, but we're not allowed to hunt them this time of year."

"Maman," Claude whined.

"It's so the mother birds can care for their young. If we kill them all, there won't be any for next year, or the year after that."

"Not allowed?" Matthew asked, "Is it actually a law?"

"It has been as long as I remember," she replied with a shrug.

Matthew glanced back at the fortress. "There are a lot of laws here that we don't have in . . . at home."

He worried about the other prisoners. Did they know about this? Claude was right; the birds were docile. He could catch them by hand if he wanted. That would be quite a temptation to the sailor hungering for fresh fowl. "What's the punishment for killing the birds this time of year?"

"It depends," Marie said. "A fine, or time in prison." She seemed to notice his dismay. "Why? What's wrong?"

"The men from the *Donna Rae*, they don't know that law. One of them could innocently break it just for a meal."

She nodded. "And when one prisoner breaks a rule, all are punished."

"They're good men, Marie—" He caught himself. "Madame Jubert."

She put her hand on his forearm. "And you worry about them."

He stared at her hand, at the long, slender fingers wrapped about his bare skin. A rush of sensations filled him. He looked up. Wide eyes stared back, as if she'd felt the jolt as well. Suddenly she pulled her hand back and squeezed it into a fist at her waist.

Matthew cleared his throat and looked around until he spied Paulette a few yards away. She had been watching them, he felt quite sure, but now she bent to study something in the tall weeds. Fleurie had dropped behind to pick flowers.

With his heart still pounding in his throat, Matthew said, "Perhaps I should go back and warn them, Madame."

"The grouse don't go into the town, and the prisoners can't come out, unless they're with their employer. It shouldn't be a problem."

Matthew still felt uneasy about the intimate moment with Marie as they walked toward the shoreline for a picnic. Occasionally he stole sidelong glances at her. What made her so appealing? Certainly she had a classic beauty, but so did many other young women. Paulette was as pretty as a spring bloom, but she didn't warm his blood the way Marie did.

He hoped that his feelings stemmed from his long months away from his friends and family, that they were a natural and temporary reaction to being away from women. No one here really knew him. Of course he felt adrift and lonely, considering his situation.

His situation. Matthew sighed, annoyed at himself. This outing was the perfect opportunity to study the outlying area around the fortress and he spent his time acting like a lovelorn suitor.

The land between where he now stood and the fortress was bare of trees. All of it would be readily visible from the battlements. It appeared that the only way to easily traverse it was over the narrow track they'd just travelled. Everywhere else was granite hillocks surrounded by soft, peaty bog. It would be nearly impossible to haul cannon within range.

He adjusted the basket on his arm and turned to follow the women toward the shoreline.

A short while later, a nasal, barking sound could be heard, faintly at first, then stronger. Everyone stopped and watched as a huge flock of geese approached from along the coastline. The giant V was only just apparent, they were so close and so many. Matthew glanced down at Claude and wasn't surprised to see the boy glowing with anticipation. It seemed as if the geese were going to land right on top of them. They circled, then jutted their long legs forward to slow the approach to land somewhere behind a stand of trees.

Claude was off. Matthew hoofed it after him, the picnic basket held in both arms close to his chest. He watched the way the boy ran and tried to leap where he leaped and dodge when he dodged. Claude obviously knew the terrain, and Matthew had no desire to land hip-deep in a peat bog. Brambles scraped his exposed shins and ankles and a branch whipped his cheek. Still, he kept up with Claude, both he and the lad whooping and laughing.

Matthew skidded to a stop and called back to Marie, "Is it legal to kill geese?"

She cupped her hands around her mouth and yelled, "Yes! Catch us dinner!"

Marie chuckled as she watched the two males disappear into the brush, one slight and gangly, the other strong and agile. Claude could use a man like that in his life, she mused, someone to hunt with him, to teach him the ways of men. Oh, if only Matthew Carter were someone else, someone Catholic and, she had to admit to herself, suitable. Her heart raced with longing.

"He's very handsome," Paulette said, one eyebrow raised in appreciation.

Marie realized that she'd been gaping at Matthew. She made a noncommittal sound. Nearby, Fleurie sat on a tree stump with a mound of yellow dandelions on her lap.

"Come along, Fleurie." The child didn't look up, so Marie said to Paulette, "She's such a dawdler."

"Did you see how strong his calves are?" Paulette continued, ignoring Marie's attempt to change the topic.

"It's from standing on a deck," Marie said briskly, "not from dancing the minuet." She pictured the king's portrait in the governor's residence. He had his calf turned so the artist could catch the hard angle of his calf.

"And that makes a difference?"

"But of course. He's most unsuitable." She frowned at Paulette. Did the girl feel the same attraction for Matthew?

"Marie, I'm only looking, enjoying him like I would a fine piece of needlework. You've no call to be jealous."

"Jealous?" Marie squawked. "I'm not jealous. He's an employee. Worse—" Her eyes widened and she looked around to make sure that Fleurie hadn't joined them yet. "A prisoner."

As soon as the words were out of her mouth, she felt ashamed. Matthew was a prisoner because of her schooner. Still, she had to keep that a secret. Paulette knew, or at least suspected, her role in the smuggling but she had tactfully never asked.

"I saw the way he looks at you," Paulette said softly. "The way a man looks at a woman he covets."

Marie felt the heat rise up her throat. "I can't help how he looks at me as long as he is respectful to me."

"Bah, you look at him the same way."

Marie stopped at the edge of a stand of pine trees, paused, then hung her head with a sigh. "Oh, sweet Mary, I do, don't I? I can't seem to help myself." Then she saw the concern in Paulette's eyes. "I have no intention of . . . er . . . . It would be wrong." *Not to mention dangerous.*

Paulette carefully set her basket on a granite out-cropping and walked over to Marie. She put her arms around her and gave her a gentle hug. Marie returned the embrace. In fact, it felt quite comforting. She'd been so nervous lately.

"What was that for?" she asked, trying to assume a matter-of-fact voice.

"It's hard having feelings for someone *unsuitable*," Paulette replied, her words tinged with bitterness. "I know."

"Oh, my dear," Marie whispered. "You do."

The previous summer Paulette had forged a friend-ship with a guard in the garrison, a handsome, friendly young man who treated her with tenderness and re-spect. They took to meeting at dusk on the ramparts. Marie had seen them there herself, two silhouettes standing close, but not touching. Unfortunately, the people in Louisbourg gossiped relentlessly about the innocent get-togethers. It was inevitable that Paulette's parents heard of the dalliance. They had the young man shipped off to Quebec.

For weeks Paulette would burst into tears at the slight-est memory. Marie came to expect her shoulder to get damp with tears whenever she saw her poor heartbroken friend. But time, she thought, had healed those wounds. Now, seeing the moisture sparkling in Paulette's eyes, Marie knew it hadn't done its job completely.

"Claude knows where we're to picnic?" Paulette asked after a moment. When Marie nodded, Paulette continued, "Then let's wait for them down there, eh?"

They collected Fleurie and hiked along the bluff until they came to the crumbling path that zigzagged down to the shore. Below them, brown- and cream-colored snipes bobbed along the mud flats, dipping their long beaks into the ooze, hunting out prey.

"Well," Marie said, swinging Fleurie up into her arms, "it's a lovely day. Let's try to leave our troubles behind and enjoy our picnic."

It suddenly occurred to her that, if her involvement with the *Donna Rae* should come to light, there would be no more perfect spring days with her precious children.

Chapter Nine

Capitaine Jerome de Monluc and Bernard Bretel stood near the wall at the top of the Dauphin Gate. Bernard leaned his forearms on the stone but kept shifting and tapping his foot, far from comfortable. Jerome had adopted his command stance: legs shoulder-width apart, spine rigid, hands clasped at his back.

"How long have they been gone?"

Bernard shrugged. "A couple of hours."

"What's he like, this Englishman?"

"He speaks French like he's right out of Paris."

Jerome lifted one eyebrow. "And that's why you don't trust him?"

"I trust my instincts, eh? Besides, why do you care? This is part of the deal: you put Matthew Carter in his place, and I spy on Marie for you."

116

"Are you sure it's not Marie you want put in her place?"

It took a moment for Bernard to answer. "When you're her husband, you can tell her what to do. Me? I'm her brother, yet she treats me like a slave. She needs to learn some respect."

"I can't argue with that," Jerome agreed. "She's a headstrong woman."

A wild woman, he thought to himself, a creature that needed to be mastered. That challenge was as great an incentive to him as the money she brought into the union.

Suddenly Bernard stepped back from the wall, as if he didn't want to be spotted. "There they are now."

They were coming across the marsh, two women, two children, and a man. Jerome couldn't see his features from this distance, but Matthew Carter looked a head taller than Marie and broad in the shoulders. He walked with the boy.

"What's Marie's son's name?"

"Claude," Bernard answered, sounding surprised that Jerome didn't already know that.

"He and this prisoner are friendly?" he asked, an edge to his voice. Marie allowed the prisoner near her son. It implied that she trusted him, and that notion made Jerome grit his teeth. The *diable* was using her son to wheedle his way into her affection. He deserved to be punished.

Bernard took a quick glance back over the wall. "Not that I know of. Claude may be only a boy, but he knows

Lynn M. Turner

how to hate the English." He paused. "It looks like they went hunting."

The prisoner had two geese, tied by their legs, hanging over his shoulder. Did that mean the man had a weapon? Surely the security in this fortress wasn't as lax as that? He would have to speak to the governor about it. Maybe they could use that as a complaint against him. No, he decided, they'd stick to the plan.

"Tell me his name again."

"Matthew Carter," Bernard replied. "He's off the *Donna Rae*."

"I know he's off the *Donna Rae*," Jerome snapped. "I'm the one who captured the smugglers."

Although Bernard gave an apologetic nod, Jerome decided that Marie's brother didn't show enough respect. Someday, when he controlled Marie's money, he would teach him some manners but at the moment he had use for Bernard.

The five people on the moor were now scouting around the ground, picking up twigs and putting them in the baskets they carried. Would Marie have Matthew carry the baskets back to the house? No. More than likely, she'd send him back to the King's Bastion and his cell. Even she didn't flaunt convention to the point where she would want to be seen with a single man, a stranger, a prisoner, a non-Catholic.

"You should go wait for him down there," Jerome said, pointing. "I want to watch you pick the fight. Make sure no one can hear you though. Just see you."

"You won't be close enough to hear?" Bernard asked, concerned.

"I don't need to hear you to be a witness. Now go."

As they neared the gates, Matthew slung the geese from over his shoulder and motioned for Claude to stop. He squatted down to be at eye level.

"You'll want to carry these yourself, yes? Otherwise people will think I killed them."

Claude's eyes were huge. "But . . . but you did."

"Bah, I wouldn't have even known where they were. You led me to them. You're a fine hunter."

As Claude shuffled and looked sidelong toward his mother, Matthew carefully placed the geese on the boy's shoulder. Their beaks hung past his knees, front and back, making it awkward to walk, but he lifted his chin and followed Marie.

Marie turned to check on their progress and saw her son. Her lips parted in a startled, grateful smile and she glanced at Matthew. Suddenly he felt his breath whoosh from his lungs. It was as if, when their eyes locked, a river of understanding flowed between them. He pictured a life with this woman, as her husband, as the father of these children. They would walk together, labor together, eat their meals as a loving family. It wasn't just a wish that he felt for a life with Marie, but a terrible need.

Marie seemed to feel the connection as well. It wasn't until Fleurie whined and tugged on her arm that she blinked and turned away.

"You'll go up this way," Paulette said, rather than asked. She gave him an intent, hard look and tilted her head toward Rue Petit Etang, the King's Bastion, and prison.

Matthew had to take two full breaths before he felt able to speak past the dryness in his mouth. "Yes, of course."

He said his goodbyes and walked slowly up the hill, deep in thought. He and Marie had been gaping at one another there, out in the open where anyone could see. He had to be more careful. She was a widow, a woman of standing in the town where gossip and innuendo were traded like currency.

And that look. Marie cared for him too. Oh, she would probably deny it, especially to herself, but her heart reached out to his. No doubt she thought of him as nothing but a crude sailor, a prisoner, because she didn't know the truth. That made their connection all the more *magique*.

Should he tell her about himself? And if he did, would she believe him? No. He would wait until his proof arrived. He didn't mind his circumstances as much as he had thought he would; he looked forward to each day of work, to the camaraderie, the honest labor, and especially the chance to see Marie. How would she react when she learned who he really was? This thought brought him almost to a standstill. She'd feel betrayed. Used. Angry. Perhaps it would help if he hinted at the truth first, and allowed her time to process it.

"You! *Garçon!*"

Matthew instinctively knew that the crude voice belonged to Bernard Bretel. He took a moment to collect himself, to assume his passive expression.

Bernard clamped his hand around Matthew's shoulder and swung him around. "I'm talking to you!"

"Yes, Monsieur?"

"What were you doing with my sister?"

Bernard must have seen them from the ramparts crowning the top of the grassy hill bordering the street. "She gave me permission to leave the town."

"I asked you, why!" he yelled.

There was more going on here than the obvious. Why was Bernard yelling? Why did he look as if he wanted to throw a punch? Matthew stepped back a pace, determined not to let the man goad him into a fight. "To carry their load, Monsieur."

"Hah! You and my sister are carrying on a sinful—"

"No!" Matthew interrupted. "Never!"

He looked around to see if anyone had heard them. A couple of people scurried by, eyes averted. He was surprised to see Paulette standing a few yards beyond Bernard's back, gaping at them.

"I've seen you leering at her."

"I'm sorry if it seemed that way. I'll take care not to look at her unless—"

"What did you say!" Bernard screeched. He shoved Matthew's shoulder roughly.

"Pardon?" He hadn't said anything to provoke this attack.

"What did you say about my sister?" Now Bernard slapped him across the cheek.

Although every fiber in his body revolted, Matthew gritted his teeth and shoved his fists behind his back. If he hit Bernard, he would be breaking the rules of their incarceration. Had the consequences been his alone, he might have resorted to violence, but he knew the other prisoners would also suffer the punishment for anything he did. Matthew stared hard at his own feet and only moved to keep his balance.

Bernard shoved him a few more times, then stopped. He squinted his eyes and seemed reluctantly to come to a decision. "Come with me."

"Yes, Monsieur." Matthew felt as if his face were made of stone. Was the man trying to get Marie into trouble? Or him? Bernard probably resented him for defending Marie that day outside Fleurie's school. But why did he make that remark about her?

The guardhouse outside the King's Bastion was a story-and-a-half stone building with a steep slate roof. Smoke poured from the blackened chimney. Three of the other prisoners stacked firewood along one wall, and two soldiers leaned against one of the arched openings to the porch, their muskets leaning within reach.

"You there!" Bernard bellowed toward the soldiers. "Arrest this man!"

"Arrest me?" Matthew gaped at him. "Whatever for?"

Rather than answering, Bernard hooked his leg around behind Matthew's knee, gave him a shove, and sent him sprawling on the hard-packed ground. He stood there glaring down at Matthew, his nostrils opening and closing like a fish gasping for breath. The soldiers approached.

"This prisoner blasphemed."

Matthew gasped. "I did nothing of the sort." He rose quickly to his feet. "Monsieur Bretel is trying to pick a fight with me, but I haven't done, or said, anything disrespectful."

The soldiers seemed to be familiar with Bernard, for they looked at one another skeptically.

"Why aren't you grabbing him?" Bernard demanded.

The first soldier scratched the short beard of his chin. "Do you have a witness to this crime?"

"I'm the witness. I told you, this man is a prisoner! You're going to believe *him*?"

"I am also a witness," a man's voice said.

Matthew saw who spoke, and his heart fell. Capitaine de Monluc claimed to witness him blaspheming, yet he had been nowhere near the confrontation.

It was a lie, of course, a conscious decision to bring disaster down upon him, and by association upon the rest of the crew of the *Donna Rae*.

At that thought, Matthew looked toward the prisoners who had been stacking wood. They stood there frozen, horrified.

Chapter Ten

Marie smiled down at Claude. His precious face was flushed, and he looked exhausted, but he continued down the alley toward the back of their house without complaint.

"We'll have to start the fire outside," Marie said. In order to pluck the geese, she would have to dip them in boiling water to loosen the feathers. The smell was revolting and she didn't want it permeating her house.

With some groaning, Claude shrugged the geese from his shoulder and dropped them onto the bench. "We can eat for a year with this."

"Very nearly," Marie said, running her hand over his head.

"I'm hungry," Fleurie complained.

"Run in and get a biscuit for yourself, and one for Claude. Then we'll get the fire going."

Fleurie pouted. "Can't we do that tomorrow?"

"No, dear. We'll want to have them all plucked before dark. You don't want to eat feathers, do you?"

"I want to go to *Grand-mère*'s house."

"Go get the biscuits and a mug of milk, then come right back out here." When Fleurie just scowled, Marie added, "Do it now."

A few minutes later, Marie stomped down some weeds that had sprung up around her firepit, a depression in her back garden. She and Claude dragged over a mound of dried branches and a couple of good-sized logs. Meanwhile, Fleurie fastidiously peeled off strips of bark and snapped tiny twigs to place at the base of the pit.

"I suppose we should wash some clothing in the water while it's still clean," Marie said.

"Why?" Fleurie whined. "None of my other friends do their own wash."

"We do it because we are able," Marie responded. "Why waste money on something we can do ourselves?"

"It's not seemly," Claude mumbled.

She darted a look at her son. "Seemly?"

"*Grand-mère* says so."

"What else does she say?"

"That we'll never make good matches if people think our mother is poor."

Even though her mother's interference made her angry, Marie kept her voice calm. "We're not poor, and people know it, yes? Besides, no one can see us washing back here."

Teanne Bretel, on the other hand, *was* poor but lived like a lady, thanks to her daughter's largesse. Marie didn't begrudge supporting her mother; it seemed her duty and she hoped, despite the loss of the *Donna Rae*, to be able to continue doing so. Part of the reason she did her own wash and cooked at the station house was to have money for her family obligations. But her mother would never recognize that. She lived to begrudge Marie and dote on her shiftless son, Bernard, and upon little Fleurie.

"I'm going to marry a prince," Fleurie announced.

"If that's what makes you happy, my sweetness. Now run along and get me the soap and the paper that the sugar cone came wrapped in."

"I'll get the water, Maman."

"Thank you, Claude."

As the children scampered off, Marie congratulated herself. It seemed they minded her in spite of her own mother's efforts.

She built the fire up, using a coal from the kitchen to light it, while Claude made trips back and forth to the well to fill the iron wash pot. As the water warmed, she shaved the soap into it.

"My dolly needs a washing too," Fleurie said, holding it out for inspection.

The dress was indeed grubby and the bonnet hung

limply over its embroidered face. A couple of Marie's own bonnets and aprons needed a wash as well, but she decided to save that chore for another day. She didn't want this water too grubby to use, after washing an armful of clothing, for the geese. Once the feathers were loose, she would perform the smelly job of plucking them.

When the back gate banged open, Marie straightened to see who had come calling. Paulette stumbled through, her face red and her chest heaving.

"Marie," she gasped. "You've got to come."

"What is it? Are you hurt?"

"The man . . . . He's in trouble."

"Matthew?" Her heart skipped.

Paulette nodded. "Bernard . . . he accused him of blasphemy!"

Claude, who had been gaping at them, relaxed and stooped to pick up the leather bucket. "He'll have to apologize to the priest, that's all."

"No, Claude," Paulette said. "This is serious. The English prisoners aren't allowed—"

"English?" Claude's voice squeaked. He turned to Marie with hurt eyes. "He's a prisoner?"

"We'll talk about it later," she said quickly. "Paulette, tell me."

"They're gathering up the prisoners and going to punish them all."

"Just like that?"

"Capitaine de Monluc claims to have witnessed the

sin, but Marie, he didn't. I was there, de Monluc wasn't!"

"Claude, take Fleurie to *Grand-mère*'s house. I'll fetch you both there later."

She ignored Claude's defiant glare, grabbed her bonnet, and headed out the back gate with Paulette panting at her side.

"Bernard should have come to me before he told the authorities. Matthew is under my supervision. I'm his employer."

"But Marie," Paulette said, "he didn't swear. I heard everything. Bernard wanted to get him in trouble. He punched him and everything, but Matthew just took it."

"Oh, Bernard! That's it. I'm not going to put up with him anymore. I don't care what my mother says."

They'd turned the corner at Rue de France and saw, up ahead, half a dozen people rushing toward the parade ground. One of them called to a woman standing in a doorway and she joined them. More people spilled from buildings.

"Where are they going?" Paulette cried.

Marie remembered the day she hired Matthew, the voice of the translator, "*For swearing or blaspheming the name of God, the Blessed Virgin, or the Saints, you will have your tongue pierced by a hot iron.*"

"Oh, no."

They were going to hurt Matthew! A wound like that could fester and kill him! Every fiber in her body screamed with the need to save him. Marie yanked up her skirts and ran as fast as she could, past houses and gardens, around wagons and carts, jumping over a child's play area. She shoved through the crowd of people, ignoring their rude comments, and took in the situation at a glance.

Matthew was chained to a pillar in the middle of the parade square; other prisoners huddled in a group guarded by soldiers with bayonets attached. The captain of the guard had a long iron poker in a gloved hand, the sharp end stuck in a portable brazier.

Seeing Matthew there so helpless and white-faced made Marie's knees go weak. She whimpered, "No! Stop!"

Matthew was yelling at the soldiers, "Just me! Only me! The others did nothing! They're good men."

But the other prisoners, who didn't understand French, looked both furious at Matthew and terrified of the poker.

Finally, Marie found her voice. "Stop!" She was ignored, so she stumbled across the open dirt circle. "Stop this madness!"

Bernard appeared at her side and grabbed her elbow. "Are you crazy, woman? Come away."

She rounded on her brother and slapped him soundly across the face. The impact sent him skidding to his side. "You!" she growled. "You are dead to me!"

She stomped up to the captain of the guard. "Release this man. He is innocent. My brother did this out of spite."

"I'm sorry, Madame, but we have a credible witness." The soldier sighed with regret. His eyes were red-rimmed from the heat of the fire.

Capitaine Jerome de Monluc strode forward with his hands open in placation. "I'm sorry, Madame Jubert, but it's true."

She wanted to slap him too. "I also have a witness that will say he did *not* take our Lord's name in vain."

As Jerome reached her, he lowered his voice. "I heard it myself, Marie. Please, come away. You don't want to witness this . . . necessary punishment."

"Liar!" She turned to the crowd. "He's a liar. I don't know why he's backing my brother, because it's just not true."

She suddenly became aware of the looks on people's faces. Avid. Pleased. She was putting on a show and they drank it up hungrily. Where was Paulette?

"Madame Jubert," Matthew said from where he was chained. "If you could just keep them from punishing the Englishmen?"

"I won't let them hurt you, Matthew." Even if Bernard did goad him into swearing, it wasn't worth this.

Now Marie turned on the captain of the guard. "And you're going to put a hot poker through this man's tongue without even a trial?"

He looked shame-faced, then nodded toward de Monluc as if to say the matter was out of his hands. "The Capitaine . . ."

"Why are you doing this, Jerome? What has this man done to you?"

Capitaine de Monluc stood to full command height. "He has taken our Lord God's name and turned it into a perversion."

"No, he didn't!" Paulette appeared from the crowd red-faced and bent from the waist. When she straightened, she looked afraid but determined. "You weren't even there. I was, and I heard everything. Bernard Bretel tried to get him to punch him, but he didn't. And he didn't swear either."

Capitaine de Monluc eyed Paulette speculatively. Then he glanced around until he spied Bernard, and gave him a quick but vicious look. Finally, he turned to the captain of the guard and said clearly, "I regret I must withdraw my complaint for fear of tarnishing these good women's reputations."

The crowd hooted and complained.

Dizziness washed over Marie. She straightened her shoulders and stared into space, praying that the humming in her ears would stop and that she wouldn't crumble to the dirt. Paulette must have noticed, because she pulled her into an embrace. Finally her vision cleared and she took a deep, fortifying breath.

"Thank you, Paulette."

"I only told the truth."

It occurred to her that Paulette's parents were going to be furious. "Perhaps you should hurry home and tell your mother before she hears it on the street."

Paulette grimaced. "We'll walk home together."

"I . . . yes . . . ."

She could feel Matthew's eyes on the back of her neck, and turned around. Although the other prisoners were huddled around him asking questions, Matthew stared at her. She felt the same tie she'd experienced earlier in the day. Although his emotions were confused and racing, she clearly read every one of them: the hurt, the relief, the gratitude, the worry, and the regret. Her heart ached to comfort him. She wanted to slide into his arms and cry on his chest.

Paulette brought her to her senses by placing a hand on her forearm. "Let's go. Bernard's coming."

Sure enough, Marie's brother bore down upon them with hate seeping from every pore of his body. Marie, weak and shaken, didn't want to face him then, and she certainly didn't intend to have him berate Paulette.

"I hope you haven't made an enemy of de Monluc," Paulette said as they strode along the road.

"I don't know what to think about that."

"He was trying to be gallant, eh?"

Marie scoffed. "That one, he can always turn a situation to his advantage. He's smart, handsome, successful. Too bad he's so mean and heartless."

"And ruthless."

Marie nodded. "I hope he's not angry with you. He said he was there, and you said he wasn't."

"I know he wasn't. I looked around for someone to help in case they got into a fight."

"Lucky you followed Matthew," Marie said, raising her eyebrow at Paulette.

"I wanted to talk to him, to tell him to take care to keep a proper distance from you." She stopped in the middle of the road. "I'm afraid you will be hurt."

Chapter Eleven

As Marie strode down the quay the next morning, she told herself that she wasn't one to care what people said, that she should simply shrug off the titters and jokes. Let the townsfolk have their fun; they would soon move on to the next juicy bit of gossip. But she couldn't ignore them. Not when it reflected on her children

Poor Claude. That morning he'd looked at her with utter disdain. That she'd formed a friendship with an English prisoner was, in his young mind, terrible. Worse still, during the picnic, she had allowed her own son to believe that Matthew was a normal person. He felt betrayed. Where had he learned such hatred for the English? He was just a toddler during the war; he didn't even remember the bombardment or the siege. Did he?

Marie knew she had to shake aside the emotions

churning within her and get on with her day. There were fishermen to feed and orders to fill. She tried to concentrate on the dinner she would prepare, and on the food in the basket that now weighed heavily on her forearm.

Would Matthew like extra leeks in his soup?

Marie stopped right there in the middle of the street and mentally kicked herself. Why did she care if Matthew liked the soup? He was nothing to her. Nothing. She closed her eyes and whispered a prayer. "Sweet Mary, please make that true. I don't want to care for this man. Nothing can ever come of it."

She slowed her last few steps as she approached the fishing property, and looked for Matthew. There he was, loading salt. He glanced up and eyed the track down the beach until he saw her. By the time Marie reached the first shack, he stood there waiting.

"Are you all right?" he asked.

"Me?" She felt taken aback by his concern. "I'm fine."

"Thank you for coming to my aid yesterday. I'm sorry you went through that. I was innocent, but even if I hadn't been . . . ." He shrugged expressively.

"I know. It was my brother's fault. I should apologize to you. And to the other prisoners. How are they?"

"Relieved. We were all terrified, I can tell you."

"I fired my brother."

Now he smiled. "So I saw. He's a hard brother, that one. And the children . . . . Did Fleurie or Claude hear about what happened?"

She'd been feeling comfortable talking to him, but

now her spirits dropped. She couldn't tell him how Claude had rebelled, how he hated the English. "I didn't hide it from them. Better they heard from me than on the street."

"At least they didn't see me . . . like that." He huffed out a sigh. "They won't understand what happened. Especially about your brother. He's their uncle. Fleurie, especially, seems very fond of him."

She couldn't help but smile faintly at his concern. He was a strong man, but sweet as well. How is it she hadn't noticed how long his eyelashes were before? Curly too. He had a small nick on his chin, probably from using a dull razor. She thought about bringing him one of her husband's, then abruptly came to herself and shook the foolish notion aside.

Just then, Jean Riverin called Matthew's name. Matthew glanced around, then turned back.

"Marie, I need to talk to you. I have to tell you something very important. About me. About who I really am."

"Come up to the door later," she said, unsettled by his expression, "when you have everything readied for the boats. We'll talk then. I'll arrange it with Jean."

He nodded briskly. "Thank you."

As he turned away, Marie asked, "Has Bernard been about?"

Matthew shook his head.

After Marie set the basket inside the kitchen and got

Suzette busy with the chopping, she went outside and waved to Jean. He wiped his hands on a rag and strode over to her.

"Have you heard what happened yesterday?"

His face was grim, and he didn't look her in the eye. "I heard."

"Jean? You didn't expect me to let those innocent men take a punishment for something they didn't do."

"It's the law, Madame. They are prisoners."

He disapproved of her. That hurt. Marie had always suspected that Jean had feelings for her, but it never interfered with their working relationship. She took his respect for granted.

"Bernard made the accusation to get back at me. It had nothing to do with . . . the prisoners. In fact, I've fired him."

Now Jean looked her in the eye. "Fired him?"

"I know you've always acted as the station master, Jean. We've spoken of it before. Now you are the station master. I will increase your bonus at the end of the season accordingly."

"Thank you, Madame. And if Bernard should come here?"

"Ignore him. Eject him. Whatever you feel is best."

Jean started to turn away, but Marie stopped him. "Has anyone gone for the bait yet?"

"No."

"Send Matthew."

"It's the job of the shoremaster."

"I need to talk to him. Please send him here before he heads out."

Jean's face closed down once again. He gave a brisk nod and returned to his work.

Matthew watched this exchange between Marie and Jean. He had already noticed that his boss was in a foul mood that morning, so he had tried to keep his distance. But after Jean spoke with Marie, he marched down to the shoreline. He was normally a placid, hardworking man, but now he looked furious. Matthew mentally braced for a fight.

"You know where we pick up the bait?" Jean demanded.

"Yes."

"When we've done the prep work, I want you to go fetch it."

"Of course."

Jean was studying his face. Finally he seemed to make up his mind. He tilted his head, motioning for Matthew to follow. Once they'd moved out of hearing range, he braced his hands on his hips and stared out to the harbor water.

"Do you remember the first day I brought you down here."

"Of course."

"I told you to stay away from Madame Jubert, yes?"

"I've done nothing improper."

Jean sighed. "That Bernard, he's a bad man, eh? He

and his sister . . . ." He shook his head. "So I believe you when you say you were innocent. I do. But there's something not right here, between you and Madame Yes?"

Matthew had spent a great deal of effort trying to appear subservient around the fishing property, especially around Marie. But now he realized that he had let down his guard. He considered slouching again, then dismissed it. "Why do you say that, Monsieur? What have I ever said or done that bothers you?"

Jean spoke toward the ground. "She looks at you. You look at her."

"I've shown her nothing but respect."

"I don't want her hurt. You understand?"

"I would never, ever hurt her."

This reply had Jean drooping his shoulders, saddened. "Now she seems to be . . . making you the master of the shoreworkers."

"No," Matthew replied. "It's not possible. Are you sure? She thinks I'm a prisoner."

"No . . . no, I'm not sure at all. She makes me feel confused."

And frustrated, Matthew thought. So he wasn't the only man around who had feelings for the Widow Jubert. He was formulating a response to this when Jean rounded on him.

"What do you mean she *thinks* you're a prisoner?"

Matthew had always known he couldn't keep up his subterfuge for long, but he had thought he'd last longer than a month. "Jean, I will explain it all to you someday."

"Explain what to me?"

"There's a ship, long overdue, but someone will come, and then I can tell you everything."

"I've always had my doubts about you. You're no sailor. Oh, you know your ways around rigging, I'm sure. And your hands were callused when you came. But you have an education. A fancy way of talking. What are you, eh? How did you land on that ship? You running from the law?"

"No."

Jean narrowed his eyes. "Maybe you're the son of a wealthy Englishman who will pay for your release?"

"I would appreciate it very much if you would keep your suspicions to yourself for the time being. Please?"

Jean brightened. "Have you told Madame? Is that why she treats you differently?"

"No, but after my encounter with Bernard yesterday, I think it's time I did."

"You will not hurt her."

"I don't want to hurt her, Jean. I really don't."

A shriveled and discolored carrot had fallen on the road. Bernard kicked it aside. He'd had enough of being pushed around by his little sister. What an insult! She thought she was some kind of holier-than-thou widow woman. Ha! She had secrets too, and he meant to find them.

He turned into Fleurie's school, scuffed down the

hall, and strode to the door where the young girls were being instructed.

The nun looked startled. "Monsieur?"

"I need my niece. Fleurie Jubert."

Fleurie raced toward him. "Uncle Bernard!"

Bernard smiled down at her pretty little face. "Come along now. We're leaving school early today."

"But Monsieur?" the nun complained. "Her mother?"

"Tell her to pick her up at her grandmother's house."

Bernard scooped up Fleurie so she perched on his forearm, and they hurried from the building.

"Did *Grand-mère* make sweets?" she asked hopefully.

"Perhaps. But first we're going to your house."

"Why?" she demanded with a pout.

"I want you to fetch me the key to the warehouse."

"It's too high. Quentin can reach it though." She sniffed. "So can you."

"This is a game, Fleurie. We're supposed to get the key without anyone else knowing. You'll have to tell me where it's kept too."

She thought about this a moment. "Is Claude playing?"

"No, just you and me."

That cheered her up. "Is there a prize?"

"What do you think?"

Bernard tickled her sides, and Fleurie giggled and squirmed in his arms. He would never understand why Marie kept this little charmer locked in a schoolroom every day. She should be outside playing, enjoying her youth. He smiled grimly to himself. He'd see that Fleurie had everything she wanted once he was in charge.

"Where is the warehouse key hanging, little one?"

"In the shop."

"Behind the counter?"

She shook her head so her curls bounced, just as she knew they would. "Up near the ceiling."

It took a few minutes to worm the information out of the child, but before they reached Marie's property, Bernard had the key's location in his mind. He just needed to get Quentin distracted for a moment so he could slip in and filch it. But how to do that without anyone knowing he was involved? He considered just saying that he needed to pick up something for the fishing station, but Quentin probably knew that Marie had fired him. Perhaps Fleurie could come for something the sisters needed at the school?

Fleurie skipped on down the lane that ran alongside the warehouse. Before she reached the gate, Bernard whispered, "Quietly, eh? We don't want Quentin to see us."

She grinned and scrunched up her shoulders. Then, with an elaborate crouch, she crept toward the gate. It swung open silently and they both passed through and down a path between raised vegetable beds. Inside the house, the kitchen smelled faintly of garlic and dusty carrots. Although the fire had burned to embers, it still hummed warmly in the middle of the room.

Through the door between the living area and the shop, he could hear Quentin moving around. Another man's deep voice was counting out money. Bernard led Fleurie back out to the garden.

"Go around to the front of the house," he instructed, "and stand across the street, eh? Call to Quentin from out there. When he comes out, tell him you came to pick up a hinge for the sisters at the school."

"A hinge?"

"He'll know what that is. When he asks what size hinge, say you forgot to bring the paper, that you'll go get it. Then hurry back here. Understand?"

She nodded and skipped up the side of the house toward Rue de Port. It was a clever plan, Bernard thought as he slipped back into the house.

Chapter Twelve

Marie's body quaked, and she wrapped her shawl more closely around her neck. She and Matthew stood, shoulders nearly touching, out of the breeze behind a derelict cabin. After hearing him speak, she felt as if every chilly drop of moisture blowing off the harbor seeped into her bones.

"Let me understand you," she said finally. "You live in France, not New Hampshire, and you *are* Catholic?"

"Yes." He looked very somber, his dark brows drawn together. "I'm telling you because I'm falling in love with you and I think—I hope—you care for me."

He was falling in love with her. Marie couldn't suppress the little quiver of joy that spurted in her heart. She squeezed her eyes shut. If only it could be so, there would be hope for them, hope that her feelings for him could be fulfilled. She shook her head, trying to take it in. "You've been pretending to be something you are not, yes?"

"Yes."

"You arrived as a prisoner and, rather than admitting who you really are, you kept lying."

He flinched at the word *lying* but nodded. "I couldn't admit it. My orders were to study the fortifications from the view of a prisoner. It shouldn't be taking so long for my real papers to reach the governor."

"A prisoner's point of view?" She heaved an incredulous sound.

"The English knew everything about us before they attacked in '45. Where the sentries patrolled, which gates were in poor repair. They had their trajectories and distances all worked out long before they sailed into the harbor."

The accuracy of the Englishmen had been a topic of conversation at the time, she remembered. "They knew all that?"

"Marie, before the siege, the British had our entire defense system drawn out, even inside the bastions; how many guns, how many men, what their living arrangements were, the munitions, even the duty rosters. They must have learned it from prisoners. A loyal Frenchman wouldn't divulge such matters."

"Any sailor visiting the port can find out."

"No civilians are allowed in the bastions or the military warehouse."

"A spy then."

He shrugged. "I am seeing what a spy could see."

"Why go to that trouble when they can interview someone who's already been a prisoner here?"

"I'm sure they've done that, but the regulations have changed since we reclaimed Louisbourg, and why would a prisoner be honest about such things? The Admiralty needs to know what's really happening here."

"They believe we allow prisoners free access?" she asked skeptically.

"As laborers, we often do. The next time, we're going to be prepared. I'll know our fortifications from their point of view. I'll know what to change, what to repair, what to move."

"The next time," Marie repeated wearily.

"There will be a next time. We can be certain of that."

"And your orders came from . . . ?"

"Directly from the secretary-general."

She heaved an exasperated sigh. "Why would he do it this way, Matthew? Or is your name even Matthew?"

"Matthieu. Matthieu Cartier. The English don't like to pronounce my name correctly—any French name correctly." Same name, different pronunciation.

She silently tasted the sound of this name. *Matthieu Cartier.* It did suit him. "I want to believe you, but . . . . I simply cannot believe that it would be worth recruiting you, and going to all this trouble."

He looked away for a moment, his arms crossed at his chest and his fingers drumming on one bicep. "It was no trouble for them. I, ah, volunteered. You see, I was coming here this summer anyway, to assume the post of first engineer to Monsieur Franquet."

"Oh, Matthew," Marie cried, holding her hands up, palms outward. That was one of the most coveted posts in all of Louisbourg. That this young man could be educated enough, experienced enough, and have the right political contacts seemed impossible. "That's even more outlandish."

"It's true. My papers, and my assistants, will be arriving on a frigate any day now. I expected them here before now." He shot a glance toward the harbor. "The plan had been that Franquet would be here before me, and inform the governor of my arrival. They were to allow me to keep my subterfuge a few days, then all would be revealed."

"You offered to be a prisoner?"

"I didn't really." Now he looked abashed. "You see, the secretary-general and my uncle know one another and, well, he was at a dinner party and, well, we drank rather a lot. He—not exactly him, but one of my friends . . ." He took a fortifying breath. "He said I didn't have the strength to survive here, that I was pampered. And Marie, I was insulted. I made a big speech, and the secretary-general, well, he suggested this route. I rashly accepted. Said it would be an adventure. Afterward, I saw no way out of it without hurting my uncle."

"Hurting him?"

"Embarrassing him. And it wasn't meant to take this long. I thought I'd spend a week or so in the prison after the arrest, and then Monsieur Franquet would come and fetch me, but he's obviously been delayed."

Suddenly Marie's breath whooshed from her. "What *arrest*?"

His face blanched. "Of the smugglers."

"On the *Donna Rae*."

"Yes."

She flew at him. "You had her taken! You! You!"

He was holding her forearms, trying to protect himself. "I'm sorry. I didn't know. I didn't understand the way things are here, that smuggling isn't immoral here. I thought—"

"Get away from me!"

She pulled out of his reach and took off away from the fishing property, away from the fortress, away from people. Now she believed him. Why else would he admit to causing her to lose so much, her very livelihood and perhaps even her children! She slowed and heaved in shaky breaths. To think that she had feelings for him! The liar! The deceitful slime! She stumbled down to the beach and dropped to sit out of sight behind two boulders. Her shoulder shook, but she fought not to cry.

"I hate him. I hate him." But she didn't hate him. That's what made it so dreadful. She loved him. The realization had her dropping her forehead on her knees. She loved him? But that didn't make any sense. She didn't want to love him. She'd been quite determined that she wouldn't love anyone.

Marie took three deep breaths, sat up straight, composed herself, and stared sightlessly across the sparkling water. What did this mean? Had anything really changed for her?

Matthew—*Matthieu*—somehow arranged for the *Donna Rae* to be seized for smuggling. That certainly explained why the schooner had been taken this time, when all the other vessels sneaking around these waters roamed freely. He wouldn't have boarded unless he already knew she carried contraband. If so, if the authorities had already discovered the *Donna Rae*'s role, Matthew didn't assume the full responsibility for the capture. That was some comfort.

It wasn't until after Matthew arrived in Louisbourg, and started working for Marie, that he learned of her involvement. He could have whispered a word to any official, at any time after that, and she would have been arrested. But he didn't. He offered to help her. He carried the message to Captain Martin.

Why did he do that? Because he had feelings for her? Or because he now understood smuggling wasn't the amoral activity that the powers-that-be in France thought? Or did he want to investigate more, to find out about Marie's partners? It hurt to believe that, but Matthew had duped her once already.

What about Gabe Martin and the rest of the crew on the *Donna Rae*? Were they thrown in prison because of Matthew? Possibly. Maybe the authorities intended to seize the schooner anyway. Maybe not. In any case, the other crew members would not look at Matthew as an innocent once they learned the truth. They'd hate him, and probably find a way to make him pay for their imprisonment.

Marie recoiled at the thought.

No one would learn it from her. Even if she wanted to get her revenge, she couldn't tell anyone and risk exposing her own involvement. She didn't understand why Matthew hadn't yet told the authorities about his so-called orders. Why did he continue to live in that awful cell? Perhaps he knew no one would believe him. Then why did she?

Oh, if only she could go back a year and decline the offer from the other owners of the *Donna Rae*. Then she wouldn't be in this financial and emotional mess. She wouldn't know Matthew even existed. She sniffed. Such thoughts didn't help.

What now? She couldn't tell anyone. Her shipment continued to be impounded. The prisoners waited for their ransom. And Matthew waited for this proof he claimed was coming soon. And if his story did prove to be true? What then? He would set up a life among the upper echelon of Louisbourg society. She would be financially ruined. Or worse. She'd see him on the street, love him from afar. And if he returned her love, what then? A thrill of anticipation rushed through her, but she quickly tamped it down. Too many obstacles loomed ahead.

Chapter Thirteen

The boy delivering the note stuck out his hand for a coin.

"Did the capitaine already pay you?" He wiggled in a noncommittal motion, but still looked hopeful. Marie said, "Then be off with you."

Marie smiled at the brazen little scamp's back as he scurried loose-limbed down the dusky street.

"What is it, Maman?" Claude asked from the hall.

"A note for me." She frowned down at the paper, cracked the seal, and scanned the writing. "Capitaine de Monluc wants me to meet with him this evening."

"That means I have to stay with Fleurie."

She bolted the shop door and returned to the living quarters as she answered, "I suppose so, for a little bit. I'll make sure Madame Saulnier is home. Why? Did

151

you want to do something? I could ask Capitaine de Monluc to come here instead."

Claude scrunched his nose in distaste. "I don't want him coming here."

"Why not?" She wondered if her son thought it improper to have a man in their quarters; his grandmother had already instilled the social moral codes and prejudices within him. "There's nothing wrong with him visiting, as long as you stay up and chaperone."

"I just don't like him."

They resumed their seats at the long table before the fire and picked up their spoons and knives. "Do you like Capitaine de Monluc, Fleurie?"

"Yuck," Fleurie answered.

Now. Marie studied her two children. How awful that she didn't know how they felt. "Why don't you like him? Was he ever nasty to you?"

Claude licked the stuffing off the top of his sweet tart. "He's mean to everybody except you, Maman. Nobody likes him."

"I suppose I knew that," Marie admitted. She just didn't realize her own children knew it.

"He's not mean to Governor Desherbier, either."

Marie chuckled along with her son. "No one's mean to him."

As she finished her meal, Marie fretted. Although worded in polite language, the note felt more like a command than an invitation. She dreaded the meeting. He wielded such a lot of power in the fortress, however, that she balked at ignoring his note. Would he ask her to marry him again? Perhaps this time he would realize the futility of his proposals. Or did Jerome plan to lecture her about her rash actions—and they were rash, she readily accepted—when Matthew was tied to the pillar?

Now she considered Jerome's ready capitulation at the square. Maybe he thought that the incident, and subsequent release of Matthew, had softened her heart to him. Or, more likely, he felt she now owed him.

A half hour later, Marie pulled on a hooded cape and headed outside. Capitaine de Monluc had indicated he would wait for her on the bench overlooking a pond. A pretty spot to visit on a warm summer evening, it promised to be chilly this early in the year. People were going to see them sitting there and assume they shared a romantic tête-à-tête.

Jerome stood like the officer he was, rigidly straight with his hands clasped behind his back. Beyond him, the approaching dusk tinted the water with a rosy glow.

"It took you long enough," he said, turning.

She frowned at his abrupt voice, and considered turning around and leaving. "We were eating when your *request* arrived."

He indicated the bench. Marie sat and arranged her skirts warmly around her legs.

"I have something to show you," he said, pulling a document tube from his inner pocket. He sat down, then handed it her.

Although she tried to keep her face blank, a clutch of
fear grabbed her throat. She untied the ribbon while
Jerome shifted out of the low shaft of sunlight so she
would be able to read.

Marie didn't need to read it. She recognized the
snapped seal, recognized the writing. With a groan, she
crushed it in her fist.

"Don't bother destroying it," he said with a snort. "I
have others. They're promissory notes for the—"

"I know what they are," she interrupted. "Where did
you get them?"

He just smiled cruelly. Marie felt her eyes glass over
with tears, and, as she didn't want to give Jerome the
pleasure of seeing them, she stood and walked forward
to the edge of the water. It felt as if she stood on the
brink of a black, yawning void. Jerome had proof that
she collaborated in the *Donna Rae* smuggling operation. He held her life in his hands. Acid rose up her
throat. She swallowed compulsively.

"What are you going to do?" she whispered.

"I don't know that I'll do anything," he said calmly
from his position behind her, still on the bench. "It depends."

She thought furiously. "Do you want a cut of my
profits?"

He barked a laugh. "What profits? I've already impounded your cargo."

She turned. "But if you release the schooner . . ."

"I might do that."

His smirk frightened her like nothing else in her life. "Or?" she choked out.

"I might take all the profits. And then some."

By his self-satisfied smirk, she knew what *and then some* meant. She looked away. "I always thought you paid attention to me because you thought I had a dowry. Now that you've seen this . . . ?" She indicated the promissory note. "And know that I'm about to be ruined?"

He patted the bench. "Sit beside me, Marie-Charlotte Jubert."

She looked around wildly, searching for some kind of distraction, some unlikely aid. But the only people in the area were strangers and, worse yet, soldiers. She slumped on the seat.

"If you will marry me," Jerome said, "I will keep this venture of yours a secret. In fact, we'll send the vessel on its way and we'll reap the profits."

"And the crew?"

"And the crew, including your precious Matthew Carter." He sneered as he spoke Matthew's name.

She bit down on her thumbnail, thinking. "I . . . I don't know. My children . . . This affects them too."

"I give you my word as an officer that I will never injure your children."

Injure them? Perhaps not. But he would likely ignore them, belittle them. Still, their futures would be secure. He might even take pride in having a son. "Why, Jerome? Why me?"

"Once the schooner is freed, you'll have money. You already have property and fishing connections. I have a station in society. Between us, we can rule here.

"What is there for you to object to? You'll live like a lady instead of a slave. Am I so hideous in your eyes? Other women seem to find me attractive."

"I don't love you." She didn't even like him.

"Bah, that's neither here nor there."

Marie thought about Matthew, and her feelings for him. Her head roared in confusion. If Matthew did join Louisbourg society . . . . Was it possible that she and he . . . No. Even if that had been possible, Jerome would never allow it to happen. He'd expose her. She was doomed. "I have to think about this, Jerome."

"What's there to think about?" he objected, his voice rising.

"My mind is spinning."

He gave her a long look, then shrugged. "Tomorrow, then."

Marie hurried back home, where she immediately checked the warehouse. The building had been securely locked, but the safe box gaped empty. She rushed to the chandlery store to make sure the key still hung in its secret place. It did, but she and Quentin would have to come up with a more secure hiding place.

Once inside her living quarters, she moved about in a daze, getting the children ready for bed, making bread and setting it to rise, and building up the fire. She was still in turmoil when she carried her candle upstairs.

A narrow hall divided the top floor of Marie's house. Two tiny rooms filled the left side, each barely large enough for the single beds where the children slept. Her own chamber took up the other side. She ducked and passed through the low door on the right, into her ten- by nine- foot bedroom with a slanted and beamed ceiling. The whitewashed plaster glowed softly in the moonlight falling through the two low windows. Lace curtains fluttered in the breeze.

The feather mattress, a remnant of her marriage days, now sagged in a single hollow along the middle. The thought of Jerome de Monluc sharing it with her brought tears to her eyes. If only she could love him. If only Matthew Carter were Louisbourgeois. Oh, but what good would that do? She'd still be in de Monluc's power.

How did he get his hands on the notes? They were locked in a safe box, hidden in the padlocked warehouse. Who knew of them? Quentin, of course, but the idea of her old friend betraying her was unthinkable. Also, if she lost her businesses, Quentin would be unemployed. She supposed that de Monluc might have threatened him, perhaps with harming one of his children.

On the other hand, Bernard would willingly make a deal with de Monluc if it meant money in his own pocket. But did he know of her involvement? He could have guessed, of course. Or gone through her papers any time in the past year. At one point, he did have access to the warehouse.

Captain Martin knew of the notes, as did the partners in New England. So did his crew.

Her fingers trembled as she worked at the linen tapes on her *jupon* and peeled off her shoes. Once she'd stripped down to her chemise and wrapped a blanket over her shoulders, Marie spread her elbows on the deep windowsill, dropped her chin on the back of one wrist, and stared out over the harbor. Pewter-colored clouds drifted against a shimmering sky, a green-blue at the horizon, darker higher up. Her schooner rode there in the middle of the harbor. She picked out the tips of its needle masts silhouetted against the shimmering water.

What would happen if she packed up her children and some belongings, and stole the *Donna Rae*? Could she concoct an escape plan with Matthew? Her eyes slid over to the *Conquerant*, a squat, heavy, ominous frigate. The darker squares on her sides were gunports, she knew. If they ever caught up to her, they'd spew liquid fire at the *Donna Rae*. Liquid fire at her children. She clamped a hand over her own mouth.

No. Her children must remain safe. Marie knew she had manufactured her own misfortune, and would have to live with the consequences. Why did she torture herself with the impossible?

She stood and moved across the softly creaking floor to the little window seat facing east. A solitary soldier walked below. Beyond him, moonlight glinted off the water. He moved along the footbridge, his shoulders bent under the weight of his musket, a lonely man doing his duty.

At that thought, Marie shook her head. Here she was feeling trapped and full of longing, but at least she had a roof over her head, one she could continue to live under if she married Jerome. Her children were healthy and well cared for. She had friends and family. That soldier, on the other hand, came from across the ocean. He shared a narrow bunk with another poor soldier, sleeping alternate shifts on the same lice-infested blankets. He had nothing to call his own, probably would never marry or have children, and likely would never even get home again.

And yet . . . .Countless times in her life, Marie had hoofed it up and down the quay. How often had she heard laughter from the taverns? Or seen soldiers lounging on the grassy bank talking companionably with one another? They survived their Louisbourg posting. They found a measure of happiness even with their pitiful situations.

Marie heard creaking from a room across the hall and soft footsteps crossing to her door.

"Maman?"

Fleurie scooted on her tiptoes across the cold floor. She curled on Marie's lap, and with a sweet sigh stuck one thumb in her mouth and twisted her hair with her other hand. Marie wrapped her blanket around the warm child and hugged her close. A marriage to

Jerome would not rob her of these precious moments. She could find consolation in that.

Marie rested her cheek on Fleurie's head and wept silently.

Chapter Fourteen

The next morning, Marie dropped Claude off at his lessons, then half-carried Fleurie up to the school. After a long, sleepless night of thinking about Jerome's coercion, she was exhausted and sad. Fleurie, who always seemed to absorb the moods of people around her, was poky and lagged behind with her lower lip jutted out.

"Come along, dear," Marie prompted. "You don't want to be late for school, do you? Or me to be late for work? The poor fishermen wouldn't have any dinner."

"You're mean to make me go to school. Uncle Bernard says so."

"Of course he does," Marie replied with a scowl. "But when you grow up, you'll be grateful."

"No I won't."

161

"Manners, child," Marie said sternly. "You don't talk to your mother in that tone of voice."

The grassy square fronting the school was dotted with children at their games: ribbons floated in the breeze, skirts billowed, high-pitched giggles and squeals rent the morning. When Fleurie saw them, she allowed Marie to give her a quick kiss on the cheek, then skipped off to join them.

"Madame Jubert?"

Marie joined the stern-faced nun who watched over the children. "Sister?"

"You know your brother took Fleurie out of class yesterday, yes?"

An instinctual terror clutched Marie's heart. "Why? You mustn't let him do that!"

Now the nun looked offended. "You never gave us those instructions. Besides, it happened so quickly, and Fleurie wanted to go." She lifted one shoulder in a shrug.

"Where did he take her?" She had picked up her daughter the same time as always.

"I have no idea. They were absent at least an hour."

Marie collected herself. Bernard, for all his faults, loved his niece. He wouldn't hurt her on purpose. But he'd be careless with her and he would—and apparently did—use her.

"Thank you, Sister. I'll speak to him. And to Fleurie."

The nun gave Marie a brisk nod, then moved off to pick up a little girl who had fallen. A few yards away, Fleurie and another little girl leaned over to poke their fingers at something on the ground. Judging by the way they both jumped back at the same time, giggling furiously, it was a bug of some sort. Marie decided to wait to ask Fleurie about the outing with her uncle. She had a pretty good idea of what had happened. It would only take a moment to confirm her suspicion with Quentin.

A few months earlier, this would have put Marie in a wounded rage, but somewhere along the line she'd given up on Bernard, given up on the hope that they'd find some common ground, given up on the dream of them being friends. They might have common blood flowing in their veins, but they were not family. With a heavy heart, she dragged her exhausted body back down to the house to talk to Quentin.

Later, as she neared the fishing property, her heart pounded and it took an effort to keep her gaze from the shoreworkers, from finding Matthew. She ducked inside the building and sighed heavily.

As always, Suzette had arrived before her to ready everything for the meal preparation. "Madame?"

The sight of the sliced bread mounded in the wooden bowl brought her up short. "Oh, Suzette, I forgot to deliver the dough to the bakery this morning."

The girl straightened. "Would you like me to go do it?"

"I'd be grateful. Thank you."

Suzette reached for her cloak. "The new *garçon* was looking for you."

Matthew. Marie dropped on a bench and rubbed her eyes. He probably thought she was still furious with him, but she wasn't. Once she had thought it through, she realized that her schooner had been identified before Matthew even boarded her. It made little difference whether or not she believed his story, since de Monluc had made his ultimatum. She would have to tell Matthew. Or would she? He'd hear about it from someone. Besides, what did she owe him? Nothing.

Why was it then, that she felt drawn to him every waking moment, the way a flower felt drawn to the sun?

"Madame?" Suzette asked, sounding concerned. "Are you ill?"

"No, just tired. Would you please ask Jean to come and see me?"

Suzette dipped her head in a yes.

As she waited for Jean, Marie gazed around the room. She should really do something; put the water on to boil at least. Everything felt wrong. She'd worked in this kitchen hundreds of times, but today her heart simply wasn't in the job. She was going to marry Capitaine Jerome de Monluc. Her face crumpled.

"You asked to see me, Madame?" Jean asked from the door.

Marie straightened and took a deep, fortifying breath. "Please have a seat, Jean. I need to discuss some things with you."

He looked disgruntled, but he sat facing her. "It's about Matthew Carter, isn't it? He's making trouble for you."

"I suppose, but not intentionally."

He leaned forward, his tanned and scarred hands flat on each of his knees. "What has he done?"

"That doesn't matter right now. None of this is really his doing." She cleared her throat. "The end result is that I am betrothed to Capitaine de Monluc."

As Jean lunged to his feet, Matthew cried from the doorway.

"No! Never!" Matthew flew forward and dropped to his knees in front of her. "You can't be serious!"

"He's right," Jean said. "The man's a pig."

Marie agreed, but now that she had made the decision, she had to adjust her loyalty, or at least the way she talked about the capitaine. "He has given me his word that he will be a good husband."

She suddenly realized that Matthew clutched both of her hands in his own. She tried to release them, but he held firmly.

"I've told you that I will make it all better," Matthew growled.

"How?" she cried. "How can you do that?"

"I'll find a way to free the—" he stopped abruptly, and looked up at Jean.

"Bah, I think I already know what you mean," Jean said, sitting down. "Madame, I saw how you changed after de Monluc brought back the *Donna Rae*. I was on the quay after you talked to him. Then you sent me to hire him." He motioned toward Matthew. "But don't worry. I haven't told anybody. I would never."

"Thank you, Jean. You are a good man." She regretted the times she'd brushed him off, and vowed to be a better friend.

Still clutching Marie's hands, Matthew shifted to sit on the bench, his leg pressed against hers. She felt his comforting warmth.

"You don't have to marry the man. You can't want to."

"I have to."

"I don't believe that," Matthew snapped.

Now Jean leaned so he was closer to Marie. "I have a solution," he said, looking nervously back and forth between Matthew and Marie. "If you were already married? I'm not a wealthy man, Madame . . . er . . . Marie, but I will always have steady work—"

She cut him off with a brisk shake of her head. "I'm very grateful, honestly, but it wouldn't solve my problems."

The big Basque man's Adam's apple bobbed up and down with an effort to swallow. He looked down at Marie and Matthew's still clasped hands. Finally, with tears glistening in his eyes, he said sadly, "I see how it is."

Marie had never seen him anything but level-headed and strong. Now she ached for him. But to show her compassion would shame him, so she tugged her hands from Matthew's and stood.

"You two better get back to work."

"Madame?" Jean asked plaintively. "There must be something I can do to help you?"

"Please." She squeezed his forearm and gave him a grateful smile.

Although Jean left reluctantly, Matthew stood firm. "Why, Marie? Was it because of what I told you?" She shook her head. "Have you already told him you'll marry him?"

"Yes . . . no . . . but I have no choice."

"There's always a choice."

"Matthew, he has proof of my involvement."

His shoulders drooped. "What proof?"

"My promissory notes. That's how I get paid once the cargo is sold."

"So this *honorable* man is blackmailing you," Matthew ground out the words.

"He promised to release the *Donna Rae*. To see that the prisoners are freed. That you're freed. No one will ever know of my involvement."

"How? He must have some hold on the governor." He shook his head sadly. "I would like the others to be released, but even after the truth about me comes out, I won't have that power. They *are* English, they *were* smuggling. As much as I regret it, I believe they will have to be ransomed as planned. I told you, I will be exonerated no matter what happens."

"And me? What will happen to me?"

"I would never tell them of your involvement."

"But the money . . . . No, this is the only way. The crew will be released; I will get my cargo back." A horrible thought had her bracing her hand on the table. "You won't tell, will you?"

"Marie!"

"I mean about de Monluc's part in the release? If you stay in Louisbourg, you'll be around him day in and day out. You'll know a secret about him."

He stared at the floor for a long moment. "Once my name is cleared, I will have some credibility." He lifted his eyes to meet hers. "You'll have to hold off the man until then."

"What good would that do? If I don't marry him, the cargo will still be impounded, and I will still be imperiled. Unless you can free her legally?"

He shook his head. "She was taken, by a naval frigate, with her hold full of contraband. I can't think of how I could." Suddenly his eyes opened wide. "I'll buy her and her contents, make the governor an offer."

"I don't think you realize the value."

He took her hands again, and pulled her to sit on the bench beside him. "Marie, I'm not a rich man. I was brought up by my uncle, and he is wealthy. Perhaps I could convince him to . . ."

She stopped his words with a sad shake of her head. "How long would that take? Six months? A year? Jerome won't wait that long." His eyebrows lowered at her use of de Monluc's first name, but she continued. "He would expose me. And even if he didn't, I'd lose my business long before then. Jean, everyone, will be out of work."

"Things are that bad?"

She nodded her head in regret. "I invested everything and then some. Two season's worth of money."

"I'm so sorry." Matthew put his arm across her back and gathered her into a hug.

"It's my own fault."

"You can't marry him," he said, his mouth against her hair. "I want you to marry me."

"Oh, Matthew."

He leaned back and tilted her chin to look her fully in the face. "I'm serious. You love me too, I know you do."

"If only . . ."

"Please don't give up on me, Marie. I'll come up with something."

She dropped her head on his shoulder. It fit there as if their bodies were built to come together as a whole. The tension drained from her neck and shoulders. When he cupped her face, she felt cherished and warm. His beautifully formed lips were so close, so tempting. How she longed to kiss him. What harm would it do? No one would see it. They had secrets between them now, what was one more? With a little whimper, she lifted her chin. Their lips met.

The kitchen, the fishing property, all Louisbourg abruptly disappeared. All that existed were her lips and his lips; her hands and his hands; her pounding heart and his pounding heart.

Chapter Fifteen

Marie didn't want to be in the house that evening, waiting for de Monluc to appear demanding an answer. He wouldn't be put off forever, she knew, but she still had some slight hope that something would happen to save her. Perhaps Matthew had come up with a solution.

She sighed. Matthew loved her. She loved him. She ran her fingertips over her lips, reliving the feel of their kiss and the salty taste of his skin. There had never been a man who moved her that way. It had never occurred to her that one existed.

The daylight lasted longer now, until well after eight. Marie bundled the children up; it would be cool and foggy damp before they returned home. They left through the back gate and meandered up the hill toward her mother's house.

She hoped Bernard wouldn't be there because she still hadn't decided what to say to him. Or to her mother, for that matter.

Madame Bretel lived in a larger house than Marie and her children, and in a more respectable area, up toward the Maurepas Gate. She wanted Marie to move there as well, but the thought of sharing her every meal with her left Marie cold. Besides, there were some excellent reasons to sit tight. A move would add fifteen minutes each way to and from the fishing property, and she didn't want to be far from the retail end of her business, for the times when Quentin needed to leave to go to the warehouse to restock. Those considerations, so serious a few months ago, now seemed trivial.

She herded her children through the front door. Fleurie scurried off calling for her grandmother. As always, Claude headed for the kitchen and the jar of sweets. Strangely, Marie's children felt more at home in this house than she did. She supposed it made sense; she hadn't grown up here, after all. That house had been destroyed in the siege, so when they returned from France they had stayed in the Rue de Porte house until her business could pay for the repair of this previously abandoned one.

Teanne Bretel sat in a rocking chair next to the iron-backed fireplace in the sitting room and gazed fondly at granddaughter. "There's my little one, my beautiful little one," she crooned.

"Hello, Maman," Marie said, entering and pulling

off her shawl. The room seemed warm and stuffy compared to the brisk, salty air outside, and moisture condensed on her nose. "How are you?"

For a moment, Teanne eyed Marie as if she wasn't sure how to respond. Clearly she had something on her mind, but she must have decided to wait to bring it up. "I can't get warm."

"Shall I make you a hot drink?"

Teanne nodded. "Where is Claude?"

"With Nadia, no doubt."

Nadia, the servant, kept the stove and fireplace humming, cooked the meals, and cleaned the house.

Teanne said, "Bring my little Fleurie some chocolate biscuits too."

The kitchen, a long and narrow room overlooking a scrubby hill, took the full width of the back of the house. Marie greeted Nadia, a thin, quiet girl in her early teens, and sent Claude back to the sitting room with a plate of biscuits. After checking that the coffee pot had been cleaned, she dipped a few ladles of water and swung the crane over the fire. The crock of coffee beans felt light, almost empty, as she picked it up.

As she ground the beans, Marie wondered where she was going to get the ready cash to keep up this household. Then, with a painful start, she remembered that she would be marrying de Monluc and therefore recouping her investment in the *Donna Rae*. Her mother would never know how close she'd come to being evicted from this comfortable home. She turned the grinder handle faster and faster, gritting her teeth.

"Are you angry at the coffee, Madame," Nadia said with a smile.

Marie's palm was red from the effort, the coffee beans all pulverized. "How is she these days?" They both knew the subject of that question.

"Something set her off yesterday." Rather than looking at Marie, the servant fiddled with the jars lining a shelf.

"The incident with the prisoner?" Nadia nodded. Marie assumed that her mother would side with Bernard on that matter, as she did on every other. "Does she think I should have let him be punished for something he didn't do?"

Nadia shrugged expansively. Then she said, "I'll finish the coffee, Madame."

"I'd rather stay and do it myself," Marie said, with a wry smile, which the servant understood. The longer she was in the kitchen, the less time she spent with her mother.

When the water had come to a boil, Marie pulled it off the heat and dumped in the ground coffee. She stirred for a bit, then shoved the concoction back over the heat.

"Has Bernard been spending his nights here?"

Nadia's face grew pink. "Yes, Madame."

That meant that Bernard had lost his room over the tavern. "He's not bothering you, is he?"

She shook her head. "He only comes here to sleep, and sometimes to eat, yes?" She indicated the crock waiting in a warm spot near the fire.

"So, he hasn't been back yet this evening." Marie grimaced. Well, perhaps her brother had found a meal elsewhere. One part of her wanted to get the confrontation over with, but the other part realized that the whole exercise would be futile. What difference did it make that she knew he had betrayed her? And why hurt her mother with the truth?

Then she asked, "I need to talk to Maman. Would you please occupy the children out here?"

Nadia leaned across the cutting block to squeeze Marie's forearm in sympathy. "Of course, Madame."

A half hour later, Marie and her mother had finished their coffee, and the children were out in the back garden with Nadine. Marie turned to her mother. "You've heard about the English prisoners?"

"About your unseemly interference, yes."

"Did you know Bernard made the accusation?"

"As was his duty." Teanne sniffed into her lace hanky.

"But Maman, they would have had a red-hot poker jabbed through their tongues, those men. All of them."

Teanne lifted her hands in a shrug. "They knew the consequence of the sin."

"That man was innocent."

Teanne's face hardened. "Your brother was there. He heard him."

"Paulette claims he did not swear."

Teanne knew who Paulette's parents were and, Marie knew, would be reluctant to speak poorly of the girl because of that. Instead, she said, "You shamed your brother in front of everyone. He will have to work extra hard to earn their respect again."

"Oh, Maman . . ." Marie rubbed her eyes wearily. Bernard had no reputation to reclaim. He was a shiftless, angry, resentful, lazy scoundrel, and everyone knew it. Everyone, that is, except his own mother.

"Besides," Teanne continued, "what business was it of yours?"

"The accused works for me."

"He's a prisoner."

"He's a good man, he—"

"How can you say that! He's English. Have you forgotten the siege? Have you forgotten how poor Yves died? Have you forgotten Paris?"

"No, Maman. Of course not. But Matthew isn't—"

"Matthew? *Matthew!* You use his first name? Have you befriended this rat of a prisoner?"

"Do not speak poorly of him. You don't know him. You don't know the full story. You may come to regret your words." Marie realized that she had growled this, so she pulled back her emotions.

Now Teanne narrowed her eyes. "What are you saying?"

"I can't tell you right now, but I will. Someday." She added *perhaps* to herself.

"All right then," Teanne drew out the words and looked at her daughter speculatively. "As long as you are not going to do anything foolish?"

Marie simply rolled her eyes at her mother. In truth, however, she'd already done something foolish. She'd fallen in love with Matthieu Cartier. She'd kissed him.

"What about the capitaine?" Teanne asked.

"What about him?"

"You're seeing de Monluc?"

"Would that please you?"

"But of course! He's a fine man."

"He's a hard person, Maman."

Teanne lifted one hand and waved it dismissively. "He's a soldier. Of course he's hard. He's a real man, that one."

How Marie wished she could confide her problems, but she knew which side of the debate her mother would take. Teanne Bretel saw only the material benefit of a situation. No one could accuse her of being a romantic. She had her soft side, of course. She loved her grandchildren to distraction, and spoiled them relentlessly as a consequence, and Marie had no doubt the devotion was real. For that, she thanked God.

"Has he asked for your hand again?"

"Maman, let's not discuss the capitaine."

Now Teanne raised one eyebrow. "He has, hasn't he?"

"I'm thinking about it."

Teanne smiled. "You better accept this time or you might lose your chance. There are other women in Louisbourg who would accept without a moment's hesitation."

"I know." Marie stood and brushed the wrinkles out of her skirt. "I better get the children home. It's past dark."

"Marie, if you refuse this time, I don't know if I can ever forgive you. Think what he can do for us, do for Bernard."

"Bernard, Bernard. All you think about is . . ." Her voice trailed off. She felt like a whining child to her own ears.

"He is your brother. He is the man of the family. Why, I don't know how you would have coped these past years if it weren't for his help."

"You are so blind," Marie snapped without thinking. "It's not as if I've kept things from you. I told you how he ran down the other property until I had to close it."

"Bad luck."

"No, Maman." She stopped. "I've explained so many times, but you don't want to hear it."

Teanne pushed herself to a stand and yanked her shawl around her throat. "It's time you married again! Past time. This preoccupation with business is . . . it's sinful!"

Marie could only snort in response. How did her mother expect the bills to be paid if it weren't for her business? "And you want me to pass the running of the businesses, as well as the ownership, over to a husband?"

"No, your brother can run them. After all these years of loyal—"

"Loyal!" Marie snapped, furious. "I'll tell you loyal. He took Fleurie out of school yesterday so he could use her to help him steal my warehouse key."

Now it was Teanne's turn to snort. "He took her out of that foolish school so she could come and visit me, her *Grand-mère*."

"Of course he'd say that to you. But I spoke to Quentin and he said—"

"Now who's blind, eh? You prefer to think the worst about Bernard. This notion of yours." She scoffed. "Bernard would have no reason to steal your warehouse key. It's that Quentin who's lost it, not Bernard."

"It's not lost. It's back in place."

"Then why?" Teanne threw her hands above her ears. "Bah, you're crazy."

"He wants to ruin me, Maman. He resents me. He always has. I'm sorry, but you know it's true."

Teanne opened her mouth to retort, but suddenly stopped. It was if she suddenly gave up fighting the battle with herself. She sat down slowly and looked toward the fire. All animation had left her face and her eyes were rimmed in red. She looked old and tired.

"Maman?"

Teanne cleared her throat. "I thought you were going."

This turn of events both worried Marie and roused her suspicions. Her mother rarely cried or angled for sympathy by showing weakness. At moments of insecurity, she generally bragged about something, or became haughty. Of course she was worried about her son, her only son. She simply tried to pretend everything was fine to hide the truth from herself.

Marie sat down and squeezed her mother's hand. "Do you think Bernard is happy?"

"No."

"You know he's not content working in the fishing business. Is there any other type of work he would enjoy more? Perhaps he could work on rebuilding the town? There's a lot of money in masonry right now."

"He doesn't want to be a mason. He wants to . . ." Her voice trailed off, and she gave her head a stiff shake as if her words were painful to air. "He wants to own a tavern."

Marie sat back. "A tavern. That's a good idea. He likes being in them. Has he tried to get work in one?"

"He doesn't want to work in one. He wants to be a proprietor. His own boss."

Of course he does, Marie thought. He wouldn't want to actually work. "How does he expect to earn enough—" She stopped abruptly at the expectant look in her mother's eyes. "Oh no, Maman. I don't have that kind of money. And even if I did, I wouldn't give it to him."

"But he seems so excited about it. As if it's just a matter of time."

So, Marie figured, in return for helping him, de Monluc had promised Bernard money to buy a tavern.

Chapter Sixteen

Marie managed to make it until Sunday without having to give Jerome de Monluc an answer to his proposal. In the intervening days, she and Matthew stole a dozen moments together in a futile search for a way out of their dilemma. All their ideas dissolved with flaws.

Now, as she and the children neared the Chapelle de Saint-Louis, and the church bells tolled deeply above, she couldn't resist looking toward the window where the prisoners were housed. No face appeared. Most of them, she assumed, would have been released for the day.

Murmurs, scuffling, and coughs hummed as the people filed into the chapel and took their seats. Marie sat on the hard bench with her children on either side of her, and her mother beyond Claude, next to the aisle. At any moment de Monluc would arrive and take his seat across and two rows up from Marie's. Tension tightened her neck muscles. She gazed forward at the brocade- and lace-covered altar. Extravagantly fat candles illuminated a massive painting above and sparkled off the gilded woodwork. It was difficult to get used to the changes made during the English occupation, such as the galleries on either side of the altar, and there had been a lot of debate about whether to remove them.

Finally Capitaine de Monluc strode up the aisle, genuflected quickly, and took his seat. He did not look around at Marie.

Father Gonillon, as if he'd been waiting for the capitaine, chose that moment to enter. He was a short man, with deeply set eyes and a dark complexion. The parishioners stilled. Even Claude, who had been kicking his feet against a bench support, stopped moving.

As usual, two altar boys led the small procession to the pulpit, rather than to the altar, and stood back so the priest could step into the raised box. He made the parish announcements in his normal, droning voice. Claude started to knock his knees against one another. Fleurie leaned her head on her mother's shoulder.

Father Gonillon paused and looked around the congregation. "And this brings me to a last, and happy matter. I wish to announce the betrothal of Marie-Charlotte Jubert to Capitaine Jerome de Monluc. If anyone has reason to . . ."

Marie jerked. Reading of the banns for her wedding? No! Horrified, she glared at Jerome. He smiled widely at her. Someone behind him reached over to pat his shoulder. Marie swung back to the priest. He must have noted her reaction because he paused and stared at her, his brows drawn together. She longed to escape, to run from the church wailing her denial. But people hemmed her in. Her mother reached across Claude and squeezed her hand, grinning broadly.

Suddenly she became aware of a commotion. People craned their necks to look toward the back of the church.

Matthew struggled with two soldiers. "Let me through!" They shoved him back toward the hall, but he fought them, searching the faces before him, looking for her. The soldiers hauled him out of the chapel and shut the doors behind them.

They were hurting him! Marie lunged to her feet, but Teanne pressed firmly on her shoulder and she sat again.

Claude pulled on Marie's sleeve. "Maman? Maman?"

Stunned, she just shook her head. People murmured and whispered all around her. They seemed to think that the man was trying to attend Mass. "A prisoner." "A heathen." He wouldn't be punished for that, would he?

"Maman!" Claude insisted in a low voice.

She looked down at her boy, at the emotions playing across his precious face: anger, incredulity, resentment, hurt. She brushed the hair from his forehead. "I never said I'd marry the capitaine, Claude," she replied softly. "He asked, but I didn't answer yet."

Father Gonillon moved over to the altar and, with the

altar boys assisting, continued with the Mass. Marie tried to take comfort in the familiar Latin words and the soothing rituals of the sacrament, but her heart pounded and her mind buzzed. She dropped to her knees and bowed her head over her hands. *Sweet Mary, Mother of God, please help us to find a life together.* The pungent incense washed over her.

As soon as the Mass concluded, Marie hissed to Claude, "You and Fleurie catch up to me outside."

She slid rudely past the people on Fleurie's left and scurried down the outside aisle. The priest hadn't even reached the back door when she burst into the hallway. She leaned into the cell, but it was empty. She brazenly asked a solder where the man had gone, the one who tried to go into the church.

The soldier waved his thumb toward the parade square. "Went to enjoy his free day, I expect."

"He's not in trouble?"

"He suddenly claims he's Catholic," he shrugged. "And it might be true, eh? He always stayed in there during this Mass. Maybe he was listening."

"Well," Marie said, relieved, "you can hardly punish a man for wanting to go to Mass."

The hall now filled with people leaving the church. Some patted her back. Others called her name. She smiled closed-lipped at them, and made vague, non-committal answers when questioned her about her be-trothal. Curious looks followed her as she grabbed her children's hands and walked across the square so quickly that Fleurie had trouble keeping up.

"Marie!" Paulette had hauled up her skirts and ran to join her. "What's going on? You can't mean to marry him."

At the sight of the horrified look on her friend's face, Marie almost lost her composure. "I didn't say yes. He tricked me. Oh, I'm in such a mess." The last words came out in a choking cry.

Paulette glanced around, saw other people nearing them, and assumed control. "Take your sister's hand, Claude," she said. "We'll hurry home ahead of you, eh?"

She linked her arm with Marie and rushed across the square.

"I'm sorry, Paulette."

"Nonsense. You did this for me often enough. You're my best friend."

"I'm sorry I haven't told you everything that's happened."

Paulette waved her hand in dismissal. "We've seen each other very little this week, yes? I'm sure you would have bored me with your goings-on sooner or later." She smiled to show she joked. Then she sobered. "I think I can guess what's happened."

Ten minutes later, the children played in the garden and the two women sat at the table with hot drinks before them.

"You've fallen in love with Matthew," Paulette started. "Does de Monluc know?"

"Not about that. At least, I don't believe he does."

"Then he's holding something else over your head."

Marie smiled for the first time. "Everyone else will think I've just come to my senses, but not you. Thank you for understanding."

"You don't have to tell me what's going on, but I'm assuming it is the *Donna Rae*."

"Jerome found out I'm a part owner."

Paulette nodded her head to show she'd figured this out already. "He hasn't had you arrested, so apparently no one else knows."

She shook her head. "I'm quite sure Bernard told him."

"You didn't take *him* into your confidence?"

"He was snooping around." She thought about how he'd used Fleurie and clenched her fists. If her daughter ever discovered the role she'd played in her mother's downfall, it would cause her pain and guilt. Then Marie would hurt Bernard. Badly.

Paulette tapped the back of her thumbnail on her teeth. "What we need is something to blackmail de Monluc with."

Marie brightened. "Do you think there's something?"

"No. I only wish there was. I'll ask my father, but . . . ." She shrugged.

"I've thought about taking the children, stealing the *Donna Rae*, and leaving. But Matthew wouldn't leave the other prisoners to take his punishment. You know how all the prisoners are punished for the wrongdoing of one."

One eyebrow shot up. "He knows how you feel about him?"

"Oh yes, you don't know who—"

She stopped, wondering how she'd explain to Paulette that Matthew was really a French citizen, that he was here to survey the fort from a prisoner's point of view. Finally, she simply repeated the story in Matthew's own words. As Marie talked, Paulette stood and paced back and forth in front of the fireplace.

"And you believe him?" she asked.

"I'm not sure if it's because I want so badly for it to be true. But I do believe him."

"I suppose it *is* possible," Paulette said, drawing out the words. "Everyone says that during the siege the English knew all about how to aim their cannons inside the walls."

"Matthew believes they learned from the English prisoners who were ransomed before that."

"But really, it's so improbable. Why would he put himself through all this?"

Marie half smiled. "He looked embarrassed when he told me the way it came about. One of those challenges that men give to one another and then are too proud to back down from. He said that he couldn't get out of it because it would shame his uncle."

Paulette digested this. "I'm sure he never expected the farce to go on as long as it has. I wonder what happened to the new engineer? The man who was supposed to have arrived before now?"

"I have a terrible fear that Monsieur Franquet's ship was lost at sea, and that Matthew won't be able to prove himself."

Matthew took up his position at the corner of the warehouse next to Marie's house and waited. It seemed so horribly unlikely that Marie had given her word to de Monluc. Especially without telling him of her intention. Something else must have happened to make her capitulate.

Birds twitted on the top of a high, slatted fence across the street. He watched them, envying their freedom. He'd been so impetuous, rushing into the church the way he had. But when he'd heard the first reading of the banns, he moved on instinct, determined to loudly proclaim that he had reason to object to the marriage. In retrospect, it was a good thing those soldiers had hauled him back.

Once again, he debated whether he should just go into Marie's house and talk to her. Then he heard Claude's voice in the garden, and realized it would be too dangerous. Marie had told him how her son was conditioned to hate the English. If he saw Matthew and Marie together, he could run to his uncle, or worse yet, to de Monluc.

Matthew understood Claude's feelings well enough.

He himself had been prejudiced, not against the English—his own mother had been British—but against smuggling, fishermen, shoreworkers, and a lot of other things that he knew little or nothing about. What a snob he'd been.

Once he assumed his real role in Louisbourg society, Matthew would work to win Claude's trust. Maybe even someday he'd earn his love. Marie couldn't marry the capitaine. She simply could not. If he lost the chance to be a father to those children, and a husband to Marie, he just couldn't see any way he'd ever feel happy again.

A half hour later, a faint pounding sounded from the other side of the block. After a few minutes of silence, two soldiers rounded the corner and strode toward Marie's gate. He thought they'd probably been knocking on the shop door, and Marie had ignored them. Matthew secreted himself in a nearby alley. The soldiers pushed open the gate to Marie's garden and entered, only to return a minute later. Why? What were they delivering? A warning from de Monluc? He tapped his foot on the ground and stared at the gate. Finally it opened, and Paulette appeared.

"Mademoiselle?" Matthew stepped from the shadow of the alley.

She pulled herself upright and stared at him, as if dithering about what to do. Finally, she approached him. "I should have known you'd be here."

"I never thanked you for coming to my aid."

She waved her hand. "I knew you were innocent. I was there."

"I saw you."

"Monsieur, I was actually following you to speak with you."

"Oh, why?"

"To ask you not to hurt Marie. But . . ." her voice trailed off, and she shook her head sadly.

"I would never knowingly hurt her."

She sighed. "Nevertheless, she's in pain."

He ached at the thought. "I want to go inside."

"It's pointless."

"She can't mean to marry him. Can't you talk to her?"

"Do you think she has a choice? That she wants to be wed to *him*?" She scowled, then asked, "Did you see those soldiers just now?" He nodded. "They came with an invitation from the governor for lunch."

He didn't understand her anger. "I wasn't aware they were friendly."

"Of course they're not. It's de Monluc's doing. He and Governor Desherbier are friendly. He'll be there, of course, the capitaine, to celebrate his betrothal with the wealthiest widow in the New World." She looked as if she wanted to hit him.

Matthew pondered how he could reach Marie on the way to the luncheon. "Will this be in the Bastion?"

"No, those chambers are still under repairs. He's

staying in the—" She stopped abruptly and gave him a probing look. "Why?"

Matthew gave his head a little shake. Someone would, no doubt, accompany Marie, so private conversation would be impossible. Then Matthew considered the governor. Perhaps it was time to meet with the authorities.

"Are his offices there as well?"

Again Paulette asked, "Why?"

"I've got to help her."

"Haven't you done enough damage?" she charged. Then her voice changed. "Oh, I know you're not responsible for the other matter, but you've made it harder. Much, much harder. If she hadn't had a real taste of love, she wouldn't know. The marriage would be a business arrangement, nothing else."

Matthew nodded, understanding perfectly. He felt the same way.

"I need to see her tonight, Paulette. Will you tell her that?"

She stared at him hard for a long time, and then turned abruptly and headed back toward Marie's gate.

Chapter Seventeen

The wind hissed through the apple tree and waves rumbled on the gravel beach a few blocks away. This late at night the town slept, except in the rowdy establishments along the quay. The places Marie avoided, the places where her brother wanted to spend his time.

Other than the firelight flickering from the kitchen window, the house looked dark and silent. Chilled, she wrapped one arm around her waist and jammed the knuckle of the other hand between her teeth. The path glowed faintly between the raised beds of new vegetable plants so she strode along them, around one, around another, around again. Her skirt made a rustling sound as she kicked it out of her way.

A creak at the far end of the alley made her freeze and stare wide-eyed into the blackness. There was a scuffing of footsteps, then a shadowy figure stepped into the faint light.

"Marie?"

Suddenly tears rose in her throat. "Matthieu."

She hadn't realized until that very instant how truly she believed his story. He was French. He was a countryman. Not that it mattered. She loved him either way.

He strode over to her, agile, broad-shouldered, smelling of salt water, peat, and tangy juniper berries. The closer he came, the weaker her knees seemed. The thin fabric of his shirt draped tantalizingly over a muscular chest and shoulders. Marie pressed her palm on the curve of a muscle and felt the give of the hair beneath. He always made her feel this way, soft and breathless.

She looked behind him. "Jean?" Matthew, she knew, would never be allowed out this late unless it was prearranged, and his employer accompanied him back to the citadel.

"Waiting on the street." He tilted his head back toward the gate.

"You and the children are alone?" he asked.

She nodded, aware that he didn't look like he had any good news.

He tilted her chin up with the tips of his fingers and gazed into her eyes. "You believe me. You called me by my real name."

"Matthieu." She remembered the first time she saw him on the fish skid, how he exuded authority and confidence. He never once looked like a subservient man. "I should have known from the beginning."

"I so regret that."

"I didn't agree to marry Jerome yet. You know that, don't you? He had the banns read without my knowledge. I would never have—"

He put his finger on her lips to stop her. "I know, my sweet. It was a sneaky trick to force you into a quick answer. I'm sorry."

His eyes glistened. Her heart ached for the remorse she read there. She said, "It's not your fault."

"You can say that? Even now? I'd cut off my own hand if I thought it could get you out of this."

"You were doing your job. I'm the one who broke the law. I knew the risks, but I took them anyway."

"Please don't marry him, Marie. Please . . ."

"Matthieu, I have no choice."

"I want you to be my wife."

Now she smiled through her tears. "It's an unattainable dream." How she wished it were possible!

"Run away with me."

"Where? And what about my children?"

"We'll take them, of course. It would just be until I can prove my story."

"It makes no difference. I will be charged with smuggling even after you are cleared of the charges."

"Only if your part comes out."

"And why wouldn't it? If I don't marry de Monluc,

he will expose me. Besides, you would never run away and leave the other prisoners to face the punishment."

He sighed heavily. "No. No. But there must be something . . . . A legal justification?"

"I have prayed and prayed."

"When I prove myself, we will take you and the children and go to France."

"I'll be married by then."

"You can't be!" he wailed. "You have to hold him off, keep a long engagement." He winced at the word.

She thought her heart would break, but she shook her head sadly. "What good would it do? The charges would follow me."

"But, Marie—"

"Please, Matthieu!" Her throat filled with tears. "It's hard enough."

"Oh, Marie," he cried, gathering her in his arms. "I'm sorry. Please don't cry. I'm sorry."

She leaned back and gazed at him. He had a tear on his cheek. She reached up and wiped it away. Her fingers shook, but she wasn't cold, not there in the shelter of his strong arms.

Matthieu kissed her forehead, her cheek, her mouth. Every nerve in her body focused on her lips. Her hands unconsciously roamed his shoulders, his chest. Finally, still breathing heavily, she pulled away.

"So you've decided not to stay here, once you're freed?"

"I will work here, but I may go back to France first, to try to find a way to pardon the *Donna Rae*. I don't know how such things work, but my uncle will. Or his friend the secretary-general might have a suggestion. I thought about writing to him, but I know he won't want something like this in writing. A matter of the heart, yes?"

"So you'll have to go all the way back to France? It's so dangerous."

"I've already sent a letter to find out where the secretary-general will be. You know, it's possible he will be in Quebec. I know he was going to do an inspection sometime this year."

"It wouldn't take so long to reach him in Quebec," she said thoughtfully.

"Can you hold off de Monluc for a year?"

Her face fell again. "No, Matthieu. He told the governor that we're to be wed in three weeks."

"You can't have agreed!"

"No, no. I talked about dresses and arrangements." She shrugged.

"You do want to marry me?" he asked, suddenly unsure.

Now she smiled. "With all my heart. But, Matthew, I will not risk my children's future. I can't risk being imprisoned, or hanged, for their sakes. Can you understand that?"

His heart constricted painfully at the idea. "I don't want you to risk that either. Never."

He hugged her to his chest. That's what he had been asking of her: to risk her life and her children's futures. How selfish. She couldn't wait until a letter came back from France, much less wait until he could travel there and make his case in person. He'd been insane to even think like that. Insane, and horribly rash. He squeezed his eyes to gather his strength, then leaned back and cupped Marie's precious face in the palms of his hands.

"I'm sorry. I was wrong to even think that way. If we can't come up with a way to clear the *Donna Rae* in the next month or so, you will have no choice but to marry him. I shouldn't have asked you to do otherwise. It was selfish of me."

"If only de Monluc didn't have such powerful friends."

"You dined with the governor. What's he like?"

She shrugged and thought about the tired man she'd seen that day. "He's not well, so I think he lets others do too much for him, make decisions that should be his alone."

"How ill is he?"

"I don't know, but he has asked to be recalled to France. I feel sorry for him. Why do you want to know what he's like?"

He rubbed a hand over his strong chin. "I will need to impress him when my baggage arrives, yes?"

An owl hooted. Matthieu looked toward the sound. "That's Jean. I have to go now."

Every nerve in Marie's body wanted to hold him back, but instead she slid out of his embrace and wrapped her arms protectively about her middle. "Until tomorrow, then." Her voice cracked so she jammed a knuckle between her teeth.

"Don't give up yet, Marie. Please."

Chapter Eighteen

Once Matthew and Jean left the waterfront the noises of town life quieted. Louisbourg slumbered except for a glimmer of reflected firelight warming windows and candles flickering on glass. Jean moved silently, his shoulders hunched, feet watching the ground.

"Thank you, for making this visit possible," Matthew said softly.

"Bah." Jean increased his pace up the hill.

"I've decided to go to the governor."

Now Jean stopped with a grunt. "This will help?"

"I don't know. I don't know." He lifted his palms face up. "If I can just convince them that Marie's schooner was helping me, working in the service of the king. Maybe they'll drop the charges."

"They won't believe you."

Matthew glanced down at his shadowed body. The hem of his seaman's trousers were a good hand's length above top of his shoes, and they were frayed and dark with stains. "No, I don't suppose they will."

Strange, he thought. At the beginning of this venture, he hated wearing the same unwashed clothing for a week. Now he kept his body and shirt fresh-smelling, but paid no notice to the stains on the fabric or the grime embedded in the folds of his skin. He'd long ago stopped thinking about such things.

Matthew touched Jean's arm to stop him. "I'll need some clothes."

"I have nothing."

"Perhaps Marie's husband's things?"

Now Jean chuckled. "He was very short. And I don't think much would have survived." He stopped and considered for a moment. "Her brother lived there for a short time. Or Quentin might have something."

"Quentin?"

"He runs the chandlery."

Matthew pictured the man: burly, clean, but hardly upper-class. Quentin had been kind to him the occasional time he'd gone to the shop to fetch things for Jean. He frowned, hating to put the man at risk.

Jean must have sensed his reluctance, for he added, "She trusts him with her life. He might lend you something; they'd fit like a sail on you though. I'll go ask Madame Jubert if she kept anything of her husband's first."

"Jean, we need haste here."

"Tomorrow," Jean said, turning around, "first thing."

The next morning, before Marie had arrived at the fishing property, Matthew found Jean in the kitchen.

"Use my room. I've left a basin of hot water."

"You've found some suitable clothing?" Matthew's neck tightened at the thought of what he would do that day.

"Quentin's daughter is a servant in a rich man's house."

"He won't notice the clothing gone? The merchant?"

"He's away."

"It's very good of you," Matthew said sincerely. "Good of all of you."

"We do it for Madame."

Although the quality of the clothing he found on Jean's bed paled in comparison to some of the attire he had worn in his uncle's home, it looked fine indeed among the rough surroundings of the fishing property.

As he prepared himself, he thought about his plan. First it required that he convince the governor that he was a loyal Frenchman, an engineer. Then came the harder part: freeing the *Donna Rae*. Without the schooner, de Monluc had nothing with which to blackmail Marie. Matthew figured that even if he could plant a doubt in the governor's mind, it could give him more time. He didn't have much faith that his plan would work, but he had to do something.

He washed lavishly and took extra care to smooth his hair before he pulled it back in a queue. Apparently the owner of the clothing was heavier in the leg, so it took the creative twist of a fishing hook to adjust the buckle so it fit snuggly above his calf. By the time he'd dressed, his hair had dried enough to powder it white.

When Jean saw him, he shook his head and said, "I wouldn't know you."

Matthew heaved a nervous sigh. "I'd best be off."

"You want me to take you?"

"No. If things don't go well, you'll get into trouble. This way I can tell them that no one else knew anything."

"They'll challenge you at the gate."

"I'll find another way in."

"There's a postern, a tunnel, not far from where they're repairing the rampart."

Matthew remembered it; he knew the prisoners working there. If this day didn't go well, the New Englanders would suffer right along with him. What would they call the infraction? Impersonating a Frenchman? Moving about the town unaccompanied? No doubt something carrying a dreadful punishment. But when he thought about Marie, he realized he would take any risk.

He shook aside that worry and said somberly, "I'm very grateful to—"

Jean cut him off with a grunt. "God go with you."

Matthew crept through the back door and skirted the

small outbuildings quickly. The road leading to the town would be busy this time of day, with people headed toward their labors, but the morning fog gave him some protection from prying eyes. The locals had become used to seeing Matthew, a prisoner laborer, but they wouldn't recognize this bewigged man. Anyone seeing him would take note, wondering who he was and what an upper-class man was doing outside the fortifications.

The Dauphin Gate now looked like a dark shadow in the swirling white. Matthew knew that a sentry would be posted there, directly under the arch. He'd seen him there often enough, with his legs straight and apart and his body leaning back slightly to support the weight of his weapon. Between him and the sentry was first an opening through the wooden stakes of the palisade, then six strides to the edge of the bridge that crossed the wet ditch. On the far side of the bridge, it took another ten paces to reach the gate and the sentry.

A sudden breeze kicked the fog apart so that the air cleared for an instant. Two scruffy men materialized. Matthew lowered his head in a regal nod. They looked just as startled as he felt, but merely mumbled a French greeting and walked past.

As soon as he reached the palisade, Matthew checked that no one was within sight, then scurried inside and veered down toward the ditch. The new grass was slimy with moisture, forcing him to brace his decent by crouching and sliding one palm behind him. He intended to follow the ditch until he came adjacent to the postern that Jean had mentioned.

Boots thumped along the bridge above his head. Matthew's heart leapt to his throat. He struggled to get under the wood.

"Halt!" a sentry bellowed. "Identify yourself." He leaned over the railing, his rifle strap hanging from his shoulder.

"Matthieu Cartier," he snapped, trying to sound arrogant and put out.

"What are you doing down there?"

"Terrible fog! Lost my footing." Making a Herculean effort to look dignified, he climbed back up the bank. A moment later he stood before the sentry.

"Who are you?" the man demanded.

"I told you. Monsieur Cartier. I have business in town."

"Who with?"

He decided try to bluster his way past. "What difference does it make?"

"Are you armed?"

"No, I'm not."

"Show me your identification."

"Bah. It's onboard the ship."

Still staring at Matthew, the sentry bellowed over his shoulder, "Guards!"

"Now wait one minute!" Matthew attempted to keep his voice level.

A moment later three other filthy, scruffy soldiers

had him surrounded. Matthew continued his arrogant stance, simply staring at them, but he recognized two of the men. He'd exchanged greetings with them many times since he arrived in Louisbourg. Terrified that they'd recognize him, he shrugged deeper into his collar. Even if they didn't recognize him, he'd be thrown in jail until someone produced his identification or vouched for him. All seemed lost when suddenly a voice called from the distance.

"Monsieur Cartier! Monsieur Cartier!" A man came jogging up the road. "There you are, Monsieur. I am so sorry. I was waiting for you . . ." His voice trailed off as he bent from the waist as if to catch his breath.

Jean. Matthew didn't know whether to be appalled or grateful. The man was putting himself at terrible risk.

"Monsieur Riverin, I thought you'd forgotten me."

"No, Monsieur. I'm sorry." Now Jean looked at the soldiers. "Pierre, Antione, Joseph. This man is with me."

"He was down in the ditch, Jean."

Jean bounced his eyebrows up and appeared to be trying to hide a grin. "In the ditch?"

"I slipped!" Matthew huffed. He strode toward the gate and left Jean concocting a story about Monsieur arriving on a ship and being ferried into the fishing property on one of his whalers. He continued the walk through the town alone.

Finally, when he was admitted into the governor's presence, Matthew found the man ensconced at the end of a long, shiny table. Centered on the wall behind him was a massive painting of the king in all his finery. Two floor-to-ceiling windows, bordered by red velvet drapes, flanked it. With the light behind him, Governor Desherbier's white wig glowed like a ripe dandelion.

Three other men sat at the table, quills poised over paper as though Matthew's entrance had interrupted their writing. Even on these clerks, lace cuffs, brilliantly white, jutted from the cuffs of fine wool jackets.

"Who are you?" the governor demanded.

Matthew assumed the aristocratic pose he'd been taught as a young lad. "I am Matthieu Simon Cartier, arrived to assume my role as engineer to the director-general of the fortifications, Monsieur Louis Franquet."

The governor glanced to the man to his right, as if to pass the discussion over to him. "We weren't informed of your arrival," the aide said sceptically.

Now Matthew noted that the other men in the room were looking him up and down, studying him. He prayed that his haughty stance hid the fishhook in his buckle.

"No, governor, and I do apologize, but I have been here for some time."

As Matthew explained the circumstances of his arrival in Isle Royale, the governor leaned back in his chair and crossed his arms over his chest as if listening to an amusing tale.

Now the aide said, "You've been spying on us."

"I've been conducting a survey of the fortress from a

prisoner's point of view," Matthew corrected. "Under the direct orders of the secretary-general."

"Show me your orders."

"I couldn't carry them on my person in case they were discovered by the enemy. Monsieur Franquet will be bringing documents to explain it all. And he will vouch for me. I expected his ship to arrive long ago."

"As did we," the governor admitted with a disgruntled glance toward one of his aides.

"He must have been delayed and unable to send word."

"You must admit, Monsieur, it is a far-fetched story."

Matthew conceded. "And yet, because of my efforts, I will provide valuable information to the admiralty and make suggestions to improve the fortifications."

"Such as?"

"We should fortify every cove, both to the east and west of Louisbourg, where a landing is possible, and keep a garrison in them." He went on to describe the heights of the cliffs and technical information about how the fortifications should be constructed.

"Anything else?"

"I think we should build a watchtower on the ridge at L'Anse a la Coromandiere."

"A watchtower?" the aide asked snidely.

"We would be able to see about four miles of the shoreline from there. Otherwise there are little coves where the enemy could make small landing parties."

"How do you know that place? Prisoners aren't allowed outside the walls."

"I worked in a fishing establishment outside the walls. Besides, I helped my employer with some heavy loads along the coast." If one could call a picnic basket a heavy load, he added silently.

The governor smiled. "You are a fisherman too?"

Ten minutes later, Matthew stood there red-faced while the governor and his men snickered and laughed at his story of how he'd been at his uncle's dinner table when he accepted the challenge to arrive in Louisbourg undercover, and how he'd been unable to get out of his promise. They had grinned when he told them how for the last few months he'd been working as the *garçon* at Madame Jubert's fishing property. Finally, the governor pushed himself to his feet. His aide immediately rose to steady him. The man appeared quite ill.

"I suggest," Governor Desherbier said, "you continue your subterfuge until Monsieur Franquet arrives. You seem to be fitting in quite well."

"I would do that, sir, quite willingly. But I have come to ask that you drop the charges against the captain and crew of the *Donna Rae*."

At that moment, a loud voice sounded from behind Matthew. "The governor has better things to do than listen to the mad ramblings of a criminal like you!"

Capitaine Jerome de Monluc strode into view, all the while looking Matthew up and down as if he were a particularly offensive animal carcass. Then he addressed the governor. "This is the man I told you about, Louis, the one I suspect is an English spy. Look at him. He stands there in his borrowed clothes looking like a tradesman, yes, but he carries himself like a soldier, eh?"

All hopes of freeing the *Donna Rae*, as slim as they were, crashed around Matthew. "I am an engineer. I can prove it to you."

"Like you just proved you've done a survey."

"Of course."

"Your survey only proves you *are* an English spy."

"If I were a spy, why would I be exposing myself this way?"

Capitaine de Monluc made a dismissive moue with his lips. "Perhaps your English confederates didn't turn up to collect you and you're feeling desperate?"

"I have no English confederates. You should know this was a set-up from the start. You're the one who arrested the *Donna Rae*. How *did* you learn we were—?"

"That's enough!" de Monluc interrupted. He bellowed through the door to the soldiers stationed there. "Place this man in irons!"

Feet thundered into the room. Matthew winced as his arms were twisted behind him. He complained loudly and bitterly, but no one listened.

Chapter Nineteen

Jeanne Bretel glowed with excitement as she looked around at the bolts of fabric and wheels of ribbons piled on every piece of furniture in her normally dour room. "What do you think of this one?"

Marie tried to appear interested, but the notion of choosing dress fabric for a marriage to Jerome de Monluc caused acid to rise in her throat. "It's very nice, Maman."

"Bah. You showed more interest when you were thirteen than you do now."

Marie closed her eyes and prayed for patience. Then she rose and walked from one bolt of fabric to the next, stopping at an off-white silk embroidered with pale pink flowers. She ran her fingertips over it, and sighed.

How she would have loved to wear this material, were she marrying Matthieu rather than Jerome.

"You like that one?" Teanne asked brightly. "It's very pretty. Shall we choose that one?"

She shook her head. "It's far too impractical. I'd never be able to wear the gown again."

"And that's such a sin?" her mother asked, rolling her eyes.

"This blue is pretty."

Teanne cocked her head to study it. "It's very plain."

"We'll dress it up with lace for the wedding. Then I can change the petticoat and remake it to wear to balls."

"Balls!" Teanne tittered excitedly. "Of course you'll be going to balls. The capitaine is a close friend of the governor's. He'll have parties for you too. It's so exciting."

Marie smiled softly at her mother's excitement. She, at least, did not consider this exercise an ordeal.

"Now . . ." Teanne rubbed her hands together. "The bigger the pannier, the better, yes?" She held her arms wide.

"Oh, Maman, the church aisle isn't wide enough for me to waddle down in something like that." Her mother's face dropped. "People don't wear those here."

"But in France they do."

"Madame?" Nadia, the servant, spoke from the doorway. "Mademoiselle Paulette is here." She motioned toward the front of the house.

"Paulette is here?" Marie said, surprised. "How did she know where to find me?"

She picked up her skirts and scurried out to the front door. Paulette waited outside on the street, slapping the side of her thighs with the flat of her hand. Marie opened her mouth to invite her friend inside, then she realized something was wrong. Matthieu? She flew down the steps.

"What is it?"

"They've arrested Matthew."

Marie didn't understand. "He's already a prisoner."

"He went to the governor this morning and told them his story about how he's really an engineer sent from France and—"

Marie interrupted. "Why did he tell the governor? Has his proof arrived? Has the director-general arrived?" She felt ready to choke with anxiety.

"I don't know about that. I just know that de Monluc was there and he said he has proof that he's a spy."

"Oh, how dare he! He has no such proof!"

"They put him in chains."

"In chains?" Marie choked. "But that's nonsense. He's not here to spy, I told you."

"You told me a story, yes. But not a likely one. No one believes it."

"I believe it! He made a rash promise and in order to keep his uncle from losing face he felt he had to go through with it. He's an engineer from France."

"You're blinded by love." Paulette gave her a pitying look and reached to grasp Marie's arm.

Marie jumped out of reach, feeling betrayed by her friend, and demanded, "Where is he now?"

"In the same prison."

"Then I must go to him."

"No! You can't. Don't you see? He's an English spy. Oh, I know you don't believe it, but if you stop thinking with your heart—"

"Ha! You're one to lecture me on that!"

She started off toward the King's Bastion, head high and stride long. If they hurt Matthew, she'd kill Jerome. Then she thought about her children. She couldn't do that to them. But she'd make it her life's work to see that the capitaine suffered for it.

"Marie! Wait! They have proof!"

"There is no proof, because it isn't true!"

"He admitted to all the plans he's made of the fortress and—"

"That was his *job*!" Marie yelled. Then she stopped and stared at Paulette, ashamed of her outburst.

"Please come back to the house. Please think this through before you make more trouble for yourself."

Marie gazed in the direction of the bastion. "What will they do to him?"

"And will the crew suffer the same punishment?" Paulette asked.

"Oh!" Marie groaned. "Poor Matthew. How he will

hate the others knowing the truth about him. If they're punished, he'll never forgive himself. Never. I can't . . . I can't . . ." Her throat tightened.

She kicked at the dirt with her shoe and thought. Who could help her? The governor? No, he depended on his aides and Jerome de Monluc to guide him, and they'd already made up their minds. What about de Monluc himself? Was there anything she could do to influence him to change his mind? No. According to him, she had already agreed to the marriage, which would mean all her earthly holdings would be transferred into his name.

Paulette was about to say something, but Marie motioned for her to stop.

Perhaps she was getting ahead of herself. She spoke aloud, "I know he's loyal to the king of France, and that he is of our faith, but the people here suspect that he's a British spy, yes? So the admiralty will want to interrogate him, maybe even make a trade with a Frenchman in the hands of the British. That will take months." Then she winced. "They won't hurt him during the interrogation, will they?"

Paulette shrugged. "I don't know."

"I have to prove his innocence. Oh, if only the ship would come from France. In the meantime, he's confined to his cell with the other prisoners—" She stopped, suddenly aware of what she'd said. "They're going to think he's a traitor. Oh please, sweet Mary, keep him safe."

"Where are you going?" Paulette called as Marie took off at a trot.

"To see Jean. Maybe we can come up with something."

"Let me understand this." Captain Martin glared across at Matthew, who hunched on the bench two treads above the damp cell floor. "You're not from a town in New Hampshire. You're not a British citizen. You're French."

"Yes." Matthew nodded his head wearily.

"And so when the governor found out, he put you in chains?" he said, his voice thick with sarcasm.

"They think I'm a British spy."

"Which," Captain Martin snapped, "would be a far safer thing to be, here in this cell."

He motioned with his head toward the window. This far into dusk, the buildings within view had become dark blocks silhouetted against a pale sky. Most of the prisoners would be trudging home from their labors. There had been no news of Jean, thankfully. Apparently no one realized that the man who was almost arrested at the gate that morning was Matthew. If they had, Jean would be in trouble as well.

Matthew felt particularly wretched when he thought about Tom Smith. Despite the differences in their ages and backgrounds, he and the old guy had become close friends these past months, spending most of their free time in one another's company, fishing, cooking over a fire, tramping about the town.

"Then there's the matter of the punishment," Martin added. "If these charges prove to be true, what will happen to the rest of us?"

"You can rest easy on that," Matthew said firmly. "The director-general will be here long before they have any sort of tribunal for me. Or you will be all be ransomed back home."

"You really believe he's still coming? You say he's months late!"

"The governor confirmed that he's coming."

"And if he's taken ill, or his ship floundered?"

"The men in the Admiralty know what I'm doing. Someone will be here to confirm my story."

"You'd better hope that legal matters move slowly in Louisbourg."

Voices could be heard approaching along the stone tunnel. "Don't say a word to my crew! Let me do the talking. I won't have blood spilled on my watch!"

Matthew shifted to rest against the stones behind him, then adjusted his chains so their weight didn't pinch the skin on his wrists. It was going to be a long night.

Chapter Twenty

As expected, the soldiers didn't release Matthew for his work the next morning. He huddled on the bench shivering; during the night someone had moved his kit bag and snatched away the tattered blanket. His shackles were attached to a loop embedded in the cement wall, making it impossible to reach his things. He waited for the day to warm.

"You've made a mess of things."

The voice started Matthew, so he jumped and rattled his chains. "Jean. Didn't they tell you I can't work today?"

"Madame Jubert told me last night." He looked angry.

"Poor Marie. I don't know how to help her now. Unless I can convince the governor to allow me to explain again?"

"What chance is there of that now, eh?"

"He must wonder why I said anything at all. Why, if my story is true, I didn't just wait for Monsieur Franquet?"

"Why didn't you say something right away? As soon as you realized that Franquet wasn't already here?"

He shrugged. "I thought he'd arrive any day. Then I met Marie . . . ."

Jean pinched the bridge of his nose. "She thinks you should ask Father Gonillon to help."

"That's a good idea. I was raised a good Catholic, you know. I've listened to the Mass from here each Sabbath." He smiled ruefully. "I'm quite up-to-date on the parish announcements, for all the good it will do me."

"Think you could convince the governor of that?"

"Not the governor, perhaps. He's ill and under Jerome de Monluc's influence. But Father Gonillon? I think I could." If he could prove that he was Catholic, the governor might give him another chance to defend himself. "Would you fetch the father for me?"

Ten minutes later, Matthew heard the priest demanding to be allowed into the cell. "He's in chains, isn't he? What could happen?"

"But he's not a believer, Father."

"I'm not sure about that."

The priest entered the cell, waited for the guard to lock the door behind him, and then approached Matthew. "Jean Riverton says you're a friend of the Widow Jubert?"

"Yes, Father Gonillon, she and I are close."

"I read the banns for her marriage last Sunday."

He felt stung again. "I heard you."

The priest studied him. "You're the one who tried to interrupt my sermon."

"I'm sorry, Father, but I when heard you, I suppose I panicked."

"I was watching Madame Jubert from the pulpit. She wasn't happy about the banns. And she almost went after you when the guards stopped you from entering."

"So you probably guessed what has happened, Father."

"I know that you went to the governor to try to get your schooner freed, but Capitaine de Monluc had you arrested. I'm just not sure why."

Matthew knew that the priest would never divulge anything he said during confession, so he shifted around to get on his knees and looked a question at the priest. "Bless me, Father, for I have sinned."

During the confession, he explained about how the *Donna Rae*'s arrest was prearranged, and how Madame Jubert was a secret owner.

"Do you think Capitaine de Monluc knows of her involvement? Is that why he captured the boat?" the priest asked.

"He didn't know at the time, but now he does. And he's using that knowledge to blackmail Marie into marrying him so he can take over her businesses." He couldn't quite suppress a shudder at the thought of the two of them together.

Father Gonillon made a disgruntled sound deep in his throat. "It's difficult to be charitable toward that man."

Matthew bowed his head again. When he finished with the list of his sins, especially lying, he asked for forgiveness. The priest gave him penance and the confession ended.

"So," Matthew said, "I would like to prove to you that I am of the faith."

"That's not necessary."

"But the governor will need proof from you, if you're to help us. Will you help us?"

"I will do what I can."

"Thank you. You know, I was a choirboy in France. I can recite the entire high Mass. Would that be enough, do you think?"

After Marie accompanied the children to their lessons, she headed back home to fetch the tray of bread loaves to deliver to the bakery and then picked up more onions and garlic from Madame Fornier to take to the station. These everyday chores seemed so tedious compared with her worries about Matthew, but she had to act as if she meant to go ahead with the wedding. Her neck tingled as if the capitaine had spies everywhere, ready to report anything she did out of the ordinary.

As she approached her own back gate, she was surprised to see Father Gonillon standing there. She'd often noticed that the man looked less impressive out of doors than he did in the Chapelle de Saint-Louis. However, today he had a determined look on his face and held his head up high. Did he intend to counsel her on marital relationships, even though she'd been married once before? Or to lecture her about something she'd done?

"Father? What brings you to my door?"

He looked around before speaking. "I'd like to discuss Matthieu Cartier."

His French pronunciation of the name had her grabbing for his forearm. "Do you know who he really is? Can you vouch for him? Did you know him in France?"

"I'm sorry, my dear, but no. I never met him before today, but I do believe he is a loyal Frenchman, and a Gallican Catholic."

"I'm glad," Marie said gratefully. She'd been impetuous to hope for more.

She reached for the latch gate. "Will you come in? The fire is still hot, I'm sure. We can have chocolate."

Once Father Gonillon was settled in the parlor, Marie left him to put the water on and arrange biscuits on a plate. Quentin must have heard her moving about because he came thundering in from the shop.

"Well? How did it go?"

"Not well, I'm afraid," she said, knowing that he referred to Matthew's attempt to get the *Donna Rae* released. "Jean told me that you arranged for the clothing. Thank you for that." She smiled sadly, grateful that she had good friends like Quentin.

"Did he accomplish whatever it was he wanted?" Quentin asked, not exactly looking her in the eye.

"He was trying to get the *Donna Rae* released," she said, hesitant to tell him more without first discussing it with Matthew. Besides, with the priest in the sitting room, she didn't want to take the time. "They charged him as an English spy."

"Awk! He made things worse, yes?"

"We'll talk about it later. I have Father Gonillon in the parlor right now."

"Oh, Marie," he said, his head tilted sympathetically, "of course. I'll leave it to you." He shuffled back toward the shop much more slowly.

She carried the tray into the other room and set it on a low table between the priest's chair and her own. Once they each had warm mugs of chocolate in their hands, she gave him a questioning look.

"I'm not sure why I'm here," he admitted. "Monsieur Cartier asked me to intervene on his behalf with the governor, but I'm not sure how to do that. Oh, I'm happy to help him, you understand, but I don't know what to say, or when, or where."

"Did he tell you his . . . of his background?"

The priest gave her a meaningful stare. "I cannot discuss what I learned in confession."

Marie smiled with understanding. "The fact that you know he's Catholic will weigh in his favor."

"Yes, there's that," he said, nodding.

She sipped her drink and thought. "Could you go to the governor with a request that Matthieu be permitted to attend Mass?"

"Yes. Yes." His head bobbed on his thin neck like a chicken pecking for food. "I feel sure the governor will believe me when I say the man is a Gallican Catholic."

"Perhaps you could ask that he be allowed to go back to work at my property, too?"

"Yes, yes, perhaps."

They nibbled biscuits and sipped their chocolate silently, each deep within their own thoughts. Marie's eyes trailed absently around the room until they fell on her late husband's books. She straightened at the thought the sight had inspired.

"I'll hire a lawyer." What difference would it make about the cost? Either she lost her businesses because she was charged with smuggling, or she lost it because she married de Monluc. Then she frowned. What would de Monluc do if he heard about her doing this? "Would you please hire Matthieu Cartier a lawyer, Father? I will pay the fees, but secretly."

"I don't believe the bishop would approve," he said with a regretful shrug. "I'm sorry."

"I understand."

"Couldn't you go yourself?"

"I'm afraid that—" She stopped, covering her mouth with her fingertips. Had Matthew told the priest about her forced betrothal?

Father Gonillon patted her hand. "To discuss your marriage contract, of course."

Her eyes widened. "Of course! He has to keep what I say in confidence, yes? Just like your confessional?"

He gave a skeptical shrug. "That is true, in theory."

After Father Gonillon headed off to try to gain admittance to see the governor, Marie slipped up to her room to change into more proper attire. She wanted to impress the lawyer with the seriousness of her problem, and to give an overall picture of financial stability. He wouldn't help her if she didn't appear to have the wherewithal to pay his fee.

Marie had passed Monsieur Berryer's office and residence countless times, as he lived adjacent to Pierre Santier's butchery. She surreptitiously glanced around as she neared, but no one seemed to pay her any heed. She tapped on the Berryers' door, leaned inside, and asked to enter.

"Madame Jubert," Berryer said, coming around his desk with his hand outstretched. "How are you?"

"Well, thank you, Monsieur." She stepped away from the open door and wrapped her arms around her midriff. "I wonder if you have a moment to discuss a confidential matter with me?"

"Of course," he said, heading toward the door. "I left this open today to let in the spring breeze, but it's really still too chilly for that, eh?"

Marie sat in a straight-backed chair and stared at her hands, unsure how to start.

"Congratulations on your betrothal," Berryer said in a jovial voice. "I suppose that's what you've come about, eh? Your contract."

"Actually, I've come about that, and another matter as well. This conversation is just between you and me, yes?"

"Of course," he said expansively.

"I mean totally confidential. You won't divulge what I say unless I agree beforehand. Understand?"

He sobered. "Yes."

She took a fortifying breath. "As you may know, I operate an inshore fishery establishment and a chandlery shop."

"Yes, of course."

"And this is the most difficult time of year for us, in terms of money. I advance the local and seasonal workers things they might need, like cordage, salt pork, biscuits, molasses . . . . They pay me at the end of the season, usually in cod."

"I am aware of this practice."

"Then I take the cod from other boats and add it to my own stock, and ship the works to Jamaica or near there."

"So it probably takes you a full year to get paid for something you've advanced in the spring?"

She nodded. "Quite so. But the thing is, the vessel I use to take the barrels south is idle a lot of the year unless I find another way to make use of her, so I took on partners in New England. That way, after we unload down south, we can bring things back to sell here and, ah, in New England."

"And this is the part you want confidential," he said with a smile.

She nodded and continued, "I thought I knew a lot about legalities of shipping, maritime law that affects me, but it occurs to me that you might see something I've missed."

He motioned to the wall of books nearby. "I keep abreast on the subject."

"There's usually no interference. The big ships that come from Europe are owned by influential people and aren't generally interfered with. It's when we offload to my vessel that I have to worry."

Monsieur Berryer tented his fingers under his chin. "I'm guessing the schooner confiscated a few months ago belonged to you."

Marie drummed her fingertips on the shiny table next to her. Once she told this lawyer the truth of the matter, it would be impossible to withdraw. If he couldn't help her and the crew of the schooner, he would be left knowing a secret about Jerome de Monluc, one he could use over his head at any time. Also, if he did decide to turn de Monluc in, it left Marie in an even more precarious position than before. In fact, he might be able to help, but decide it would be in his best interest to use her information against her.

Marie always detested being in someone else's debt.

Then she thought about Matthew and how life would be without him. Her fingers stilled.

"Partially, yes," she finally answered, "It's one of the things I wanted to talk to you about. To see if there's any way that she can be released."

"Why didn't you come to me earlier?"

"Because I didn't want anyone to know of my involvement. I was smuggling, and the *Donna Rae* was captured, so I didn't think there would be any way you could help."

"Has that changed?" he asked, eyebrows raised.

"Things have gotten more complicated." She paused, unsure how she could—and even if she should—tell him about de Monluc blackmailing her.

"How was the schooner arrested?" he prompted.

She exhaled. "You may want to arrange to talk to Captain Martin in person, assuming we can find a way for you to do so without arousing suspicion."

"For now, tell me what you know."

She briefly explained the arrangements she'd made the previous winter, the bills of exchange with her partners, and how the goods reached the Isle Royale shores. "They reconnoitered in a small bay just south of Canso, and loaded there, in the sheltered waters."

"It's a remote bay?"

"Oh yes, very private."

"So there were no witnesses?"

"Not that I know of, but apparently Capitaine de

Monluc had prior knowledge that she would be there. He was waiting outside the mouth of the bay. He allowed the large ship to leave, but arrested my schooner. She had her hull full of contraband."

"Contraband?"

She listed some of the cargo. "Furniture, nails, rice, axes."

"Hardly the sort of goods our administration usually concerns itself with."

"There was someone, a man, on board." Marie sat up straighter. "I want to tell you about a friend of mine, Matthieu Cartier."

Chapter Twenty-One

Matthew didn't know whether to be grateful to Marie for arranging a lawyer to visit him, or angry at her for putting herself at risk.

"So you didn't actually go ashore?" Monsieur Berryer asked.

"Not for days. Why? Do you think we can use that fact? Perhaps since we never actually touched French soil?"

A bell gonged above, and the lawyer pushed himself away from the wall he'd been leaning on, as if ready to go. "I've never heard of that happening, so I doubt it."

"Will you leave those books with me for a bit?"

He frowned and glanced at the empty fireplace. "I suppose so."

"And speak to Captain Martin?"

"Oh, perhaps, perhaps. I don't want to waste my, ah," he paused and glanced toward the door, "my client's money. I'm sorry, but there it is."

After the lawyer left, Matthew pushed himself back against the wall and arranged his chains so they didn't weigh down his arms. He ran his hands over the marbled paper that decorated the cover of the heavy tome. *Maritime Commerce*. He knew a great deal about how to calculate the weight of a slate roof, or the distance between two points of land, but next to nothing about maritime law. And he didn't have time to learn. Nevertheless, he opened the book to the table of contents and began.

An hour later he heard the lock turn in the cell door and Captain Martin shuffled in, shaking himself like a wet dog. "Bah, I don't know why they want to live here on this barren rock. Terrible weather."

Heavy rain slanted through the grates of the window, leaving an arc of dark stone on the cell floor where it reached. Matthew glanced at the cold grate longingly. "Think they'll let us have a fire?"

"I'll go back out and forage for some wood," Captain Martin said with a grimace. "Wish I'd thought to do so before."

"There's a good spot for driftwood where the shore curves down by Madame Jubert's." A person had to get there early in the day, before other people picked the area clean.

"Yeah, well, I suppose you'd know that."

Matthew nodded, sorry he'd brought her name up. In the last few days, the other prisoners had given up being overtly angry with him, but their moods hadn't thawed either. They didn't know whether to be mad at him because he was a French spy, or because he pretended to be a French spy.

"What have you got there?"

Matthew hoisted the book. "Maritime law."

Captain Martin lifted an eye. "Where'd you get that?"

"Borrowed it from a lawyer. I don't think I'll be able to make sense of it. I'm not a lawyer."

Captain Martin sat beside Matthew and asked softly, "Did someone hire you a lawyer?"

Matthew nodded. "I pray *he* doesn't find out about it."

That was all it took for Captain Martin to understand that Marie had hired the lawyer. "Too bad I don't read French."

Matthew brightened. "I do. Maybe you could tell me what to look for?"

"Shouldn't you be trying to find out about a different kind of law? Treason and that sort of thing?" He sounded disgruntled and suspicious. "You can be sure that our owners are already searching for legal loopholes to get the *Donna Rae* back. If your story's true, all you have to do is wait for that ship to arrive."

"That'll take too long." When Captain Martin just sniffed and looked away, Matthew added, "You don't want her to marry that man any more than I do."

"True," Captain Martin conceded.

That evening found Captain Martin and Matthew both huddled together with their single candle illuminating the law book. The other prisoners sat around silently listening to the exchange and occasionally making suggestions.

"I don't see why we're at the mercy of French law in the first place," Tom Smith said with a huff. "We never once touched their cursed shoreline."

"They figure the waters near to the shore are theirs too," Captain Martin replied.

"No," Matthew said slowly. "You're brilliant, Tommy."

Tom replied with the first smile he'd given Matthew in three days. "Figure you can get us an English law book?"

"We don't need to. We didn't break any English laws."

Captain Martin looked doubtful. "Are you saying the French don't claim the inshore waters as their own?"

"I don't know. We'll have to look here."

Five tense minutes later, Matthew repeated what he'd just read, "Cannon distance from shore." His heart began to pound. "We were in a big bay! In the middle of it."

"We passed through the narrows to get into the bay. That's less than three miles."

"But our holds were empty then."

"They were full when we left."

Matthew smiled. "But we weren't on board then. Capitaine de Monluc's crew sailed here."

Marie sat stiffly on the edge of a hard chair in her mother's parlor and eyed her mother, talking to Jerome de Monluc. They looked like the enemy to her, plotting how to get her in prison more quickly. Jerome appeared to thoroughly enjoy Teanne Bretel's company.

He turned to Marie. "You never told me your mother was so charming."

She smiled at him through gritted teeth and thought, *Why don't you marry her then?*

"And you say the governor himself will attend the reception," Teanne gushed.

"He wouldn't miss it."

"Imagine, Marie," Teanne said, "the governor. Such an honor."

When Marie didn't respond, Jerome looked at her speculatively. "You're very quiet, my dear."

Earlier in the evening, Marie had decided that the safest course of action was for her to keep her mouth closed, so she simply shrugged and picked up her coffee. Her mother had arranged the visit and tricked her into attending. At least Bernard wasn't at home. That would have been too much to bear.

Teanne tittered. "She's a blushing bride! Look at her color."

"Very becoming," Jerome agreed.

He reached over and clasped her hand. She froze, and stared down at his short stubby fingers, deeply tanned with blackened nails.

"What do you say we get married this week, my dear?"

She yelped. "This week? *This* week! No . . . no . . . . We can't be ready, right, Maman? It's impossible."

"I think it's a delightful idea," Teanne squealed.

Marie jerked her hand free from Jerome's. "No, it's impossible. The banns . . ."

"Bah," he scoffed. "They're just custom. There's no one who would object to our union." Now he bared his teeth at her. "Is there?"

She faltered at the hard look in his eyes. "Father Gonillon would never agree."

"I'll pass a little money over his palm to convince him."

"No! He'd be insulted."

"Then we'll find a different priest."

"We can be ready by Friday and—"

"No, Maman!"

"Nonsense, the dress is almost finished. And you're the one who only wanted a few guests."

Jerome reached over and squeezed her leg, hard. "Friday. It's settled."

Teanne clapped her hands together. "Oh, it's so exciting."

Suddenly, bile rose up Marie's throat. She scurried out of the room and lurched down the hall to the kitchen, where she dropped onto a stool and buried her face in her hands. Her whole body shook with the sobs.

"Marie?" Bernard emerged from the pantry.

"Oh, go away."

"You're crying. I don't think I've ever seen you cry before."

She was too desolate to register his quiet tone at first,

but then she glanced up at her brother through blurred eyes. He looked confused.

"You must be very happy," she gulped out.

"I . . ." He tilted his head, thinking. "I thought I would be." He turned around and walked out the back door into the darkness.

A moment later, her mother came into the room. "What is the matter with you, child?" She paused, probably when she realized that Marie had been crying, then she clicked her tongue. "Wash your face and get back into the parlor. We have a lot of planning to do."

"I can't, Maman. I'm not feeling well."

She made an exasperated sound. "Then your betrothed will walk you home. But come here first thing in the morning. Do you hear me? We'll hire a runner to deliver the invitations—thank goodness Jerome has a large receiving room—and visit the dressmaker to get the hem, and—Marie, where are you going?"

Marie headed toward the back door. It felt as if every muscle in her body had hardened. She needed to see her children right away. She needed to be reminded why she had agreed to this horror. How could she live knowing that her marriage bound her to Jerome but her heart belonged to Matthew? Oh, Matthew, if only. If only.

Teanne followed her to the door. "We have a lot to decide."

"You decide."

"This is insufferably rude!" Teanne called. "Come back here! At least let him walk you home. Marie, stop!"

Chapter Twenty-Two

Paulette sat quietly in her chair in the lawyer's office and listened while Captain Gabe Martin explained their legal position to Monsieur Berryer. He spoke with an accent, of course, but his words were perfectly understandable, so she felt only frustration that the lawyer kept shaking his head, dismissing everything before he'd even heard the lot.

Although only she and Captain Martin sat, Father Gonillon and Jean Riverin stood behind her, ready to add emotional support, if not actual words, to the discussion. The four of them radiated determination, but Monsieur Berryer still shook his head.

"I would be wasting my time," the lawyer announced.

"But we weren't smuggling. If anyone was, it was Capitaine de Monluc."

"That's not the way the court would see it." Monsieur Berryer turned to Paulette. "You know this. You understand how things work. Your own father—"

Paulette held up her hand, partly to silence him and partly to give herself time to collect her thoughts. "Yes, I do know how things work. That's why I know that it's not whether the courts would rule in our favor—although I feel sure they will, if it comes to that—but that the governor believes it is possible that they will. He's not the kind of man to make unnecessary trouble for himself."

Berryer stuck a finger under his peruke, behind his ear, and scratched so his wig jostled. "You want me to take this directly to the governor?"

"But of course." She shrugged. She had thought about simply asking for an audience with him directly, but having a lawyer present gave their position more weight.

"Mademoiselle, I'm not sure you understand how difficult it is to reach him."

"Pfft." She swatted the notion away as she would a fly.

"Not today, he won't. He's ill, you know. But perhaps his secretary?"

She gave her head a delicate little shake. "It must be the governor, and right away."

"Mademoiselle, you are very persuasive, but I still don't see why he will listen to you. If he wants to know about the arrest, he has only to ask his friend Capitaine de Monluc."

Gabe Martin said, "I doubt that de Monluc gave him the actual details of the arrest because, once he thought things through, he must have realized he was hasty in boarding us."

The lawyer nodded, one eyebrow raised. "And what's to stop him from lying about it? Huh?"

"But his crew? They know what happened."

"And they know that your intent was to smuggle, so it's all a thread in the same cloth to them."

Father Gonillon cleared his throat. "If the capitaine wanted to release the *Donna Rae*, he'd only have to admit to having made a mistake, yes?"

Paulette swung around and looked the priest in the eye. Apparently he was already aware that de Monluc was blackmailing Marie, and that he intended to free the schooner after they were married. And he would release her, so he'd be able to reap Marie's profits.

"You're right," she drawled. "He must already know he made a mistake. How else does he think he can release the *Donna Rae*? Legally, that is?"

"And he does mean to free her," the priest agreed.

They turned and stared at Monsieur Berryer. He gave each of them a careful study. "So," he finally said, "we're all reading off the same page here, eh? We know what the capitaine plans to do, and why."

Suddenly Captain Martin stood and shoved his chair back out of the way. "The scoundrel," he snarled. "He's been letting us fester here all these months. Why, I bet the owners have already written and demanded our release on these very grounds!" He slapped one fist into the other palm. "I wondered why it was taking so long."

"Wouldn't your owners' letter go to the governor?" Monsieur Berryer asked.

"Easy enough for de Monluc to intercept it. He hangs over the man's shoulder most of the time anyway. I can just hear him: 'Here, Louis, let me handle this little matter for you.' "

The captain looked so fierce that Paulette felt like shrinking away from him. "If this is the way it happened, then we have to expose him."

Monsieur Berryer said, "He's going to be exposed anyway, when either a letter reaches the governor, or the schooner's representative appears here in Louisbourg. No matter what the timing of the release, de Monluc will, eventually, admit that he made a mistake in the manner in which he arrested the ship."

"He's been pushing for a hasty wedding. Maybe he knows someone is on his way," Paulette said, her stomach tightening.

For the first time, Jean spoke up in his Basque accent. "She has to call off the marriage, or at least postpone it!"

"He'll immediately turn her in," Paulette answered.

"But when the schooner is released?" Captain Martin asked. What then?"

"*If* the schooner is released," Monsieur Berryer replied. "As I said, this is a flimsy legal argument. It will work for de Monluc, who only has to make it so, but I'm not sure it would work for anyone else. Once the *procureur du roi* begins legal proceedings, de Monluc will lie about where he arrested you."

Marie ached to see Matthew, and even headed over toward the bastion after she dropped Fleurie off at the school, but she forced herself to stop. If de Monluc heard that she'd visited the prison, he would make Matthew's situation even worse. She turned on her heel and marched off in the opposite direction.

When he wasn't at sea, de Monluc spent his days going between the barracks, the governor's offices, and the quarters he rented in a huge house overlooking the ocean. She whispered a prayer that he wouldn't be at home at this time of the morning, and started up the hill. As she approached his impressive front entrance, it occurred to her that Jerome might expect her to move the family up here. She found the idea distasteful. Such a waste of money. How did he, a mere naval officer, afford such luxury anyway? Was he in debt? Is that why this marriage was so important to him?

She took a deep breath and climbed the eight broad steps. Should she knock on the door? Why? Didn't a betrothed couple go in and out of one another's homes without ceremony? She tried the lever handle and found it locked, so she knocked anyway.

A pretty and very young maid answered the door. She looked terrified when she saw Marie, and curtsied three or four times as she stammered, "Madame Jubert. Madame Jubert."

"As you know who I am," Marie said with a kind smile, "you must know why I'm here." She passed the girl and entered a gleaming foyer.

"No, Madame."

"To inspect the house for the wedding reception."

The girl glanced down at her apron where a smear of what looked like dark batter marred the otherwise stainless cotton. "We are preparing the food right now."

"Ah, yes," Marie said, with a regal nod. "Then you must go back to the kitchen. I'll just see myself around."

"I'll fetch the housekeeper, Madame."

"That's not necessary."

Marie felt like tiptoeing around the rooms but forced herself to act like the future mistress of the place. The thought that she would marry Jerome in one day's time still seemed impossible, even though she could think of no way out of it. It loomed there like a guillotine ready to fall.

According to the maid, at least one other person toiled below. Their services weren't free. Yet no one ever talked about Jerome's family or his background, or his personal fortune, so how did he afford to live like this? It looked more and more to Marie like the pretentious de Monluc lived way beyond his means. The fact that he kept even the whiff of the possibility of such a scandal from public gossip spoke volumes about the power he wielded in the town.

If Jerome was nearing financial ruin, she needed to know now, before she turned her estate over to him. Where would he keep his personal papers?

Although the house was sparsely decorated, each piece of furniture looked expensive to Marie's untrained eye. High ceilings, vast windows, dark paneled walls, a few carpets here and there. The fireplace was of carved marble. She passed quickly through the salon. When she came upon his desk, she gave a furtive glance around to assure herself that no one had arrived, and bent over the secretary. The front dropped down to expose an untidy mess of papers, soiled blotters, a block of wax, and jars of ink. She went through them quickly: drafts of Admiralty letters and reports, a couple of undecipherable lists, nothing important. She hoisted the drop-down back in place and reached for the cupboard below. Locked. She felt around the top part of the secretary again, in the grime of the corners and the paper dust, but found no key. Undeterred, she poked around inside the keyhole with a penknife, but merely dulled the blade tip. Finally she slid it carefully down the crack between the door and the desk, next to the keyhole. It clicked open.

Ten minutes later, Marie-Charlotte Jubert moved like a driving, roaring storm in full fury. Still yards from the governor's apartments, she hollered to a guard. "Find Capitaine de Monluc and bring him to me!"

He looked taken aback at her barked command, but quickly recovered. "I'm sure Madame would like to wait—"

"Bring him to me immediately! Now go! Go!"

She halted at the foot of the stairs, fists on hips, foot tapping rapidly on the cobblestones. One of the town's wealthy matrons drew near, but Marie snarled at her so obviously that the woman's eyes widened and she made a wide circle to pass.

"Marie?"

"Paulette? What are you doing here?"

Paulette swept down the few steps to join Marie. "We're trying to get an interview with the governor."

"Who is?"

Paulette waved behind her where Father Gonillon, Monsieur Berryer, and Jean Riverin were emerging from the building.

"We have an idea, Marie. We think we might be able to help you."

Marie looked from them back to Paulette and then back to the men. Were they there on her behalf? No, that was too much to ask. Wasn't it? Her anger at de Monluc deflated as she considered what these people, two of them her dear friends, were doing. Could it be? She felt humbled.

"Why are *you* here, Marie?"

With a start, Marie remembered the papers she had stuffed into the pocket hanging from her waist. "He knew all about it," she said, her ire rekindled. "That pig."

Paulette scrunched up her shoulders in anticipation. "About the illegal arrest?"

"Huh?"

"They took the *Donna Rae* too far offshore to make the arrest legal."

"Oh . . . oh . . . oh." Marie scrambled to dig out the papers. "Now I understand what this means. He was told to do that so that they could release the schooner after Matthew had a chance to do his job."

"De Monluc knew Matthew was French!" Paulette gasped.

"Yes! When Monsieur Franquet realized he'd be delayed, he wrote to the governor and explained everything, but the letter obviously never got to him." She shook the papers in the air.

"Well!" Paulette chirped, her face a mix of outrage and joy. "Let's go show him."

"The governor? No. I want to make Jerome release the prisoners, and acknowledge Matthew, without mentioning me to the authorities at all. And I'm keeping some of this proof of his treachery as assurance that he won't try to hurt me or mine ever, ever again."

"And he'll call off the wedding?"

She assumed a pinched-nose voice. "Jerome de Monluc will announce that he has decided to return to

France because of his many unpaid bills, and that I have decided not to marry him."

Paulette grinned. "Very gracious of you."

By now, the three men had joined Paulette and Marie on street level.

"Let me get this straight." Monsieur Berryer said intently. "The Admiralty office arranged for Matthew Carter to be aboard a schooner that they knew would be smuggling. They ordered Capitaine de Monluc to arrest her in international waters so the charge could be easily dropped. But de Monluc kept this intelligence from everyone here."

"So he could force Marie to marry him," Paulette snapped.

"He needed my estate because he's in financial ruin," Marie added.

"He is?"

"Oh yes. And I have proof that he's been speculating on illegal shipments as well. Not successfully, either." Now she grinned.

Capitaine Jerome de Monluc appeared at the doorway and looked down at the five of them. He must have seen by their smug expressions that something was amiss because when Marie unrolled the letter from France and held it up, he clearly guessed its contents. For a second, he looked ready to bolt. Then his shoulders dropped, and he swore in defeat.

* * *

Marie hurried toward the King's Bastion, followed by de Monluc, soldiers, and a gaggle of curious people. As they approached the guardhouse, and saw the soldiers there react to their approach, it suddenly hit her.

Matthew waited behind that massive wall. In chains, yes, but only for a little while longer; the governor had ordered that all the prisoners be released immediately. She moved out of the way and felt behind her for the smooth planks of the bridge railing. Her legs felt as wobbly as a codfish.

What if Matthew didn't feel as she did? What if he'd been saying those things about loving her and wanting to marry her because of the unreal circumstances of his life? Maybe when he thought things through he'd reconsider. She squeezed her mouth with her hand.

Feet thundered over the drawbridge. Voices echoed through the passageway. Everything about her buzzed with excitement and activity. But Marie held her breath and waited.

Suddenly, he was there, tall and handsome, searching over people's heads, until he caught sight of her. She whimpered.

"Marie," he said. "Marie, it's true?"

Emotion blocked her words, so she nodded.

"You're free?" he asked again. "Free to marry me?"

"If you still want me?" she croaked.

"Oh, my love," he cried, gathering her into his arms. "Always."

* * *

By August of 1751, Capitaine de Monluc had vacated his fine house in Louisbourg and moved to, rumor had it, the wilds of the north country to work off his many debts. According to a poorly written but friendly letter that Tom Smith had sent to Matthieu, the captain and crew of the *Donna Rae* were safe at home in New England.

In early September, Marie-Charlotte Jubert and Matthieu Cartier stood before their friends and family in the Chapelle de Saint-Louis and spoke heartfelt vows of marriage. Afterward, they traveled in a laughing procession to the gardens adjacent to the residence of the new governor, Monsieur le Comte de Raymond. It was a warm, soft night and Marie felt as if she walked on floating feathers.

Triple lanterns twinkled high along the walls of the garden. Harpsichord and violin music chimed sweetly. Servants stood behind linen-covered tables heaped with food and drinks. And everywhere people smiled and laughed.

"I'm sorry Gabe Martin can't be here," Marie said.

Matthieu pressed a kiss to her forehead. "But all our other friends are here."

"I've never seen Jean Riverin in formal attire before." Marie smiled fondly at her old friend.

"He's never smelled better either," Matthieu joked. "I think your mother bathed him in rose water. He probably prefers the stink of salt cod."

"You smell pretty good yourself," she said, nuzzling

under his chin. "Are you getting used to wearing your own clothes again?"

He shrugged. "The fishermen dress more comfortably, that's for certain."

Marie sighed contentedly and scanned the garden. "Maman is quite taken with your boss, yes?"

"What? With Louis Franquet?"

"See them over there?"

Teanne Bretel coyly covered her mouth with one hand and looked up at the chief engineer through fluttering lashes. Nearby, Bernard watched over Claude and Fleurie and the other children.

Just then, the musicians launched into a minuet. Three handsome officers jerked as if they were puppets on a string, then rushed toward Paulette to be the first to ask her to dance. Quentin Bauldry bowed to his wife and led her onto the green.

"Will you dance, Madame Cartier?"

"With you, Monsieur Cartier, I will dance my life away."

"I love you so much," he whispered.

"Ah, Mattheiu, I will love you forever."